THROUGH THEIR

Eyes

Through Their Eyes

Edited by Amanda Deed, Cindy Williams and R. A. Stephens, 2023
Stories are © to individual authors.

Cover Layout by Carmen Dougherty.
Layout by Rhiza Press.

978-1-76111-115-0

Published by Rhiza Press, 2023
PO Box 302,
Chinchilla QLD 4413
Australia
www.wombatrhiza.com.au

THROUGH THEIR Eyes

EDITED BY
Amanda Deed,
Cindy Williams &
R.A. Stephens

rhiza press

Contents

Is This How it Ends? 1
  Emily J. Maurits

A Change of Allegiance 16
  Deborah Henley

City of Bees 24
  D J Blackmore

Changing of Season's Hues 43
  Elaine Hartskeerl

Yana's Song. 58
  Ruth Corbett

The Gift 78
  Wendy Adams

A Refuge for Yitzhak 86
  Amanda Deed

My Brother's Keeper 104
  Valerie Volk

L'Mort de Lazaraus 114
  V. M. Cherian

Faith Like a Child 124
  R. A. Stephens

Claudia Procula 130
  Laura Motherway

Burdens 139
  Anne Hamilton

Murder at my Feet 155
  Cindy Williams

Meet the Authors 174

Is This How it Ends?

Emily J. Maurits

So Noah came out, together with his sons and his wife and his sons' wives. All the animals and all the creatures that move along the ground and all the birds—everything that moves on land—came out of the ark, one kind after another. Then Noah built an altar to the Lord and, taking some of all the clean animals and clean birds, he sacrificed burnt offerings on it. The Lord smelled the pleasing aroma and said in his heart: 'Never again will I curse the ground because of humans, even though every inclination of the human heart is evil from childhood. And never again will I destroy all living creatures, as I have done. – Genesis 8:18-21

Tirzah scanned the horizon as the sky grumbled. Where was Japheth, her husband? Behind her milled the rest of the family, attempting to build shelter for their first night on land, a task much hampered by the swaying gait they'd all acquired after over a year on the water. More worrisome than their sea-legs, however, was the threatening mass of clouds above them. It had ceased raining months ago. Why did it look like it was about to start again?

As fear churned inside her, Tirzah made an impulsive decision to believe the unrealistic, the unlikely, the impossible. Maybe the absence of her husband and the colour of the sky were not linked. Maybe no one had sinned.

He'd just gone to collect firewood, after all. Going to find timber wasn't the same as fleeing from judgement. It wasn't. Yet, Tirzah had to admit, it looked similar enough, especially while they were all still balanced on the uncertain razor edge of a new world. And so, rather than hunting through the terrified eyes of her family for an encouraging expression or a concessive smile, she'd retreated to the edge of the camp. These were the facts: the sky was primed for a deluge and Japheth was missing.

What should she do?

She spared a glance for the mountain towering behind them, and imagined she could see Noah trekking up its heights with wood on his back and fire in his hand. A man on his way to commune with his Creator.

In reality, she could see nothing but a dark smudge beneath a furious, water laden sky. And reality brought back past reality, and suddenly all she could see, feel, breathe, was crushing, swirling water, bloated bodies and the salty-sour smell of fear.

Tirzah swallowed against her growing terror, her heart expanding into her throat. Could this coming storm really be Japheth's fault? She tried to think logically. If he had offended God, why would he run? The flood had proved that God could see into all hearts and the reaches of his power knew no bounds. All things were his to destroy and to save. You couldn't run from God. Besides, why wouldn't Japheth have *told* her? Evil lurked in all their hearts, she would not have judged him for it.

That thought acted like a catalyst to her fears. Was each sin to be punished with a flood? If that was the case it was only a matter of time. Even if it was Japheth today, it could just as easily be her fault tomorrow, or Ham or even Noah. How many times can a world be destroyed? How could they possibly live with the terror of righteous judgement always hanging over them?

Overwhelmed, Tirzah latched onto her one uncomplicated thought. Japheth was missing and she needed to find him. She broke into a run.

The mud slid between the soles of her feet and her sandals, but she pushed forward, flinging her arms out to counterbalance the motion. There was a shout behind her, and she charged towards the line of dark trees, tunic flapping, desperate to reach the wooded shelter before anyone tried to stop her. Something in the sky rolled over and over, as it had before the rains began all those weeks ago, and once more her heart clambered its way into her throat. *Was this really the end? Saved only to be destroyed? What was wrong with them? Why couldn't they last even a day in this new world? Why couldn't they be good?*

She heard the sound of breathing to her right and, thinking it was a family member trying to herd her back to safety, she forced her leaden thighs higher, swinging her arms harder. Almost there.

Crack. Her right foot slid out to the side, and the ground came up to meet her, the force shuddering through her palms into her elbows. Mud beneath her nails, hands burning, Tirzah rolled, struggling to raise her head off the ground, struggling to be ready to meet her pursuer.

'Woof!' Tongue hanging out, breathing heavily, the dog snickered.

Tirzah sank back. 'You!' She managed, and without thinking held out her arms. The dog bounded forward, as he had so many times when they'd been fellow refugees in their wooden world, the universe melting outside. Tirzah buried her suddenly stinging eyes into his black, shaggy fur.

For a second.

'Poo! You smell!' She shoved him away gently, and he smiled at her, legs coated in mud almost up to his chest. She looked down at her own feet and noted the snapped rope on her right sandal. It was too short to be tied, so she kicked them off and staggered upright, wincing as her feet, softened by their voyage, met the spiky new grass and the silty soil.

'I have to find my husband Japheth,' she told the dog. 'If he did sin, maybe there's something we can do. If not, he must be hurt. He went out to gather firewood ages ago.'

Tirzah stepped into the undergrowth, but the trees weren't old enough, weren't tall enough, to remove the threatening, olive coloured sky from her vision. She pushed down a bolt of panic. First things first. She had to find her husband. If she couldn't save him, well, at least they would die together.

Swollen, torn bodies. Gaping mouths. Hands still outstretched. A child-sized bow and arrow floating in the dirty water. Bedraggled land birds, bodies limp and too small, too pliant.

'Woof!'

Tirzah shook herself and looked down.

'Woof!'

'Still here?' she asked the black dog gambolling at her feet. 'I don't have any food.' She showed him her grazed but empty hands. 'We're out of the ark now. You need to find your own. You can go back to being your own master.'

The dog grinned, tongue lolling past its chin.

Tirzah walked on.

***

The first drop was like a burning brand. It landed on her forehead and set her entire body alight. She broke into a run. It was happening. It was happening. The sky was opening once more. The water was falling.

Screams. Sheer, unadulterated panic. Entreaties. Threats. But what was far worse: the crushing truth. The creatures are against their Creator, and now the Creator is against his creatures. What hope is there to discover in a cosmos like this?

Drop. Drop. Drop. The rain was falling steadily now as she charged through the undergrowth. Faster, faster, as if she could outrun judgement and tumble into hope. The leather tie that held her hair fell out, and the long strands began whipping her shoulders in time with her strides. She had to find Japheth before the rains began in earnest.

Water kills fast, and this water comes down from the heavens in deafening sheets and heavy waves. No one outside the ark stands a chance: prediction and promise meet. The world ends in bloodless unconsciousness, Noah's offer of mercy echoing tardily in its ears.

Where's the warning this time? Tirzah thought, as she wove through the trees, eyes searching left and right for any glimpse of her husband. How can we hope to survive the next flood without a warning? *Oh God, send a warning! Give us a chance to make it right.*

Pitter patter. Pitter patter. The rain, her feet, her breaths, her hair, her heart – the tattoo was all-consuming. The rain, her feet, her breaths, her hair, her heart. The rain, her feet, her breaths, her hair –

'Argh!' Tirzah's bare foot struck a rock, and she pitched forward. This time her body was too exhausted to roll, too unfit after so long in the ark, and she landed heavily on the ground. Her open mouth filled with sodden debris. She lifted her chin and spat once, sand crunching between her teeth. Then she slumped back, closing her eyes against the rain.

Did it matter if she found Japheth? Soon the waters would reach waist-high and there would be no hope for any of them. Did it really matter if her husband had sinned in his heart, or her, or another family member? Perhaps this time only Noah and his wife would be saved. A cold realisation spread across her shoulders and down into her stomach. God had not needed to save the whole family. One man and one woman was enough to recreate the Garden, to begin again. Two of every animal, but so many more humans. Why? Because God knew they would do evil so soon and he wanted to make sure there were enough to survive this second flood? Is this how it ended for her? For Japheth?

'Urgh!' Something cold on her cheek. Tirzah opened her eyes, only to have them filled with slimy, warm tongue. 'Eek, get off!' She shoved the dog away and sat up, wiping her sticky hair from her face. At once she realised just how much dirt she still had in her mouth, and began spitting, summoning what saliva remained after her run to try and expel every last grain.

The dog laughed.

Tirzah rolled onto her knees, heedless of the mud and dirt which now caked every inch of her. She wished she had another leather band for her hair. She let the rain collect in her palms, but it wasn't enough to properly rinse her mouth or even to wash her face. *Strange. It had been heavier last time.* The thought only brought more fear. Death comes easier when it comes in a rush.

The dog's fur was flat and oily beneath her fingers, but she embraced his soaking, squirming body in the hope that his mammalian warmth would somehow penetrate not only her skin, but her thoughts as well.

The rain came down, and she hugged the wet dog and wondered if this was a little bit, just a little bit, like it had been in the beginning. She'd grown up with the stories, of course. They all had. Passed down from mother to child, like an ember which refuses to go out, in the hope that one day it would ignite again.

Eve had been, the tales whispered, the mother of stories. In the final years of her life, she had spent hours each day telling her children and grand-children and great-grand-children everything she could remember about her life before. She told them what the rough tongue of a lion feels like, when it licks your hair in the heat of the day. She showed them, with her words, how cheetahs and gazelles had once danced together over the plains, each feeding vicariously off the others' speed, running faster and faster until their dappled bodies were a joyous blur. She wove into their blood the comforting heat of the dragon's breath on their foreheads, the lilting laugh of the hyena when it lies beside you in the shade, the lipping bubble-mouths of the salmon nuzzling your calves in the water. She gave them the world she had lost them that day in Eden. She gave it to them in bright story fragments, which, until the flood, had remained ghosts just out of reach, summer daydreams, nothing more.

Then the forced cohabitation in the ark, the tentative melding of animals and humans once again. Two of every kind (although, for many this did not last long. The mice, particularly, tended towards expansion), and a chance to discover which animals held onto a remnant of Edenic friendship, and which retained, instead, their Edenic speed, or vitality, or cunning.

Dogs, she'd learned, had held onto the former, cats the latter.

Tirzah pushed her cheek against the wet dog's fur and breathed in its awful scent. 'Is this how it's going to be?' she asked softly. 'Even now we've left the ark? Will your kind stay near to mine?' She licked the rain droplets off her lips. 'It would be nice.'

It would be more than nice. It would be like living, for a little while, for a few encounters out of every day, in one of Eve's stories. It would be like carrying around a little parcel of Eden, a broken ember of light in a smelly coat and an over-enthusiastic tongue.

'Woof!' The dog shouted. 'Woof!'

And, though cold, dirty and afraid, Tirzah laughed. 'Come on, love,' she said, getting to her feet, blinking against the rain which still hadn't quite developed into flood strength. 'We have a husband to rescue.'

Instead of smiling, the dog stiffened, nose pointing to the left. The rain was too loud for Tirzah to hear its growls, but the sharp outline of its front legs told her all she needed to know. She bunched her smarting hands into fists and turned.

'Ah –' she swallowed her cry of shock almost immediately, her heart acting as a natural gag, but it was too late. The bear rose onto its hind-legs, stocky body towering above the recovering shrubs. Tirzah did not move. It had been obvious to the whole family that whatever had imbued the animals with a certain degree of Edenic peace for the length of their voyage had quickly dissolved upon landing. Gone was their rough and tumble floating oasis, and with it, whatever gratitude the Creator had enabled his animals to feel.

What *this* animal felt was obvious to Tirzah. Its squat nose wrinkled in hunger, frustration and fear. She slowly took a step back. Come with me, dog, she begged silently. Come with me. *Back down!*

The dog's hackles rose as its mouth dropped into a toothy snarl. Tirzah looked around for a stick, a rock, anything. Just as she was concluding that not only was there no weapon within grabbing distance, but that she stood very little chance of winning any fight even if there *had* been one, three things happened at once.

The bear dropped down onto its four paws and leapt towards her, the dog sprung in between them, barking furiously, and a bright light exploded into her vision, startling her into action.

She ran.

Tirzah ran like she'd never run before, pelting through the undergrowth, sliding on wet ground, sodden clothes slapping and chaffing. She also prayed like she'd never prayed before, begging the Creator for the smelly lump of Eden she'd left behind to fight a bear on her behalf. She ran and she begged, feet going on, prayers going up.

Please let Japheth be safe.

Please give us a warning.

Please save the dog.

Please save us all.

Please stop the rain, just this once! Just this once! We're not good, but we will be. We'll be good, I promise, I don't know how, but oh God, we'll be good.

Oh God, let us be good.

On and up. On and up. On and –

'Tirzah!'

She almost didn't stop, the new voice merely one more sound to escape, one more premonition of disaster. But names hold power. They anchor people to reality, identity, even when all seems lost. They too, are one more ember of Eden, where Adam and Eve knew and were completely known.

Tirzah remembered herself and, sliding on the mud, tried to look behind every tree in one wide sweeping gaze. 'Hello?'

'Tir –'

She saw Japheth before he could even finish, saw him in all his familiar, comforting glory, and then her eyes filled with tears.

'Oh! Oh!' She flung herself in the direction of her husband, knee-caps cracking against the stony soil, and tried to touch all of him at once. It wasn't difficult, for Japtheth was sprawled on the ground, one arm holding himself up, feet stretched out.

'Tirzah, oh thank our God, oh thank our God –' He flung his free arm around her neck, so her head was pulled towards him by the crook of his elbow. She shoved herself roughly into him, and their cheeks met with a wet slap, her chin sliding down his hairy jaw. Salty skin on salty skin, the same raindrops tumbling over them both. They were as physically close as two people could be and it wasn't close enough. They breathed.

'How did you find me?' His lips spoke into her hair, his voice muffled, scratchy.

She pulled back, but only enough to read his expression. The rest of her continued to soak in the comfort of his skin, just as he bathed in hers. 'Why didn't you come back?' she demanded. 'What's happened? Did you cause the rain?'

'What?' The rain was making clean conduits over his dusty skin, and his normally curly hair was flat against his forehead. 'No! I thought someone else must have done something.' He held her gaze, and she could see that they both understood. *This was it.* There has been no warning this time. This would be the flood they wouldn't survive.

His Adam's apple tightened, saying everything that needed to be said, and then he went on. 'I fell, and I hurt my heel and now I can't walk for long. I have to keep resting. It's going to take me a while to get back.'

She turned her attention to Japheth's swollen foot, although apart from making a sympathetic noise in the back of her throat, she couldn't think of anything else to do. Although keeping him pinned to the rock studded ground probably wasn't particularly helpful. Tirzah released him and rolled, but although his arm tumbled from her neck, finding her palm, he rolled with her. They remained entangled on the forest floor.

It was as good a place as any to wait for the end of the world.

Silence. She'd been able to squash her fear while she'd been focussing on finding him, but now his hand was clenched in hers, Tirzah began to shake. What should they do now, while they waited for the waters to rise? She wanted to tell him about the dog, and the bear, and the way Noah had disappeared to speak with God and hadn't come back yet, her fear about the evil in their hearts, but she couldn't quite find the words. Should she start with the dog or her suspicions? Perhaps there really was nothing to say. What use are words when there's no one to keep them? Why place meaning into a world that is about to be destroyed?

It hit her then that perhaps Eve's words would die with her. Of course, whichever human pair God chose to rescue this time around would tell the stories still, but if that pair wasn't her and Japheth, then *she* never would. Never again would the beauty of the garden, the darkness of the lies, the fracture and reconciliation between Eve and Adam play over her lips. She'd tell no more stories of the Creator walking with his creatures, no more tales of hope in the face of shame, no more promises of redemption lurking on the horizon.

Tirzah swallowed, but couldn't quite manage to push down her post-adrenaline despair. Eve's stories had kept her alive, kept them all alive. Perhaps more so than the ark itself, because what is an ark without a God to shut its door and keep it floating? That's what she'd really miss, Tirzah thought, if she and Japheth weren't chosen. More than her husband, more than her family, more than the dog, more than running through gullies on windy days or telling stories by the fire, giving voice to the murmurs in their shared blood.

If she and Japheth weren't chosen, she'd miss her God.

'Tirzah! Tirzah!'

'Hmm?' she wiped her eyes.

'Look!' Her husband squeezed her hand, his other arm

pointing to the sky. 'Look!'

She sighed, knowing he was trying to cheer her, and glanced up reluctantly, only to freeze. 'What *is* it?'

'I don't know. It's like... it's like... a bow and arrow. Without the arrow.' He tilted his head in a way which made her fall in love with him all over again. 'And with more colours.'

She stared up at the colourful arc in the sky. 'The rain's stopped!'

Japheth held out his hand, as if to check, but she didn't need his confirmation. She remembered the sudden flash of sun behind the bear's head in the clearing. Even as she'd been running in terror, God has been at work. The rain had slunk away. It had stopped before the water had gotten waist high, head high, flood high. It hadn't even reached her ankles!

The storm had passed. Was such a thing possible?

'What does this mean?'

'Mercy! Reprieve! Forgiveness!' Japheth burbled as he spoke, struggling to contain his laughter, rubbing a hand through his wet hair in disbelief. She fell back against him, tension sliding from her body, leaving her heavy and disorientated.

'How – how do you know?'

'Well,' Japheth sobered for a moment. 'I guess we'll have to see what my father says when we get back. But the rain has stopped! And what better sign of peace than a bow without an arrow? Look at the colours! Who places such beauty in a sky about to be obliterated?'

Could it be true? Tirzah squinted up at the reds and yellows, the greens and pinks. In their forest clearing weak sunlight bounced from glistening leaf to sodden tree, and above them the clouds had softened into mauves and almost-transparent greys. Was that a streak of blue on the horizon?

Did you hear us God? Do we really get a second chance? A third chance? A fourth chance? Is this a sign of something good, or a warning?

Tirzah wanted more than anything to believe that the colourful stripe in the sky was a sign of blessing, a sign of hope, a sign of mercy. With her husband laughing helplessly beside her, she could almost believe it was.

Almost.

Oh God, show me! Show me that Eve's stories hold something real.

The prayer took the final ounce of her strength. She pulled her hand from her husband's and brought her trembling knees up to her chin, using both arms to keep them there. Her head ached, and she let it fall, all her bruises crying out at once. She licked her scaly lips.

'Tirzah?' Japheth flopped down, flat on his back, arms behind his head, gazing at the sky beatifically, still panting in happiness.

'Tired. Thirsty.'

Show me, God.

'Tirzah? I think we should – ah!'

The underbrush exploded, and a little ember of Eden burst through, tail wagging, mouth smiling. Tirzah found the energy to open her arms and the dog leapt into them, dragging his tongue over every inch of skin he could find. Her searching fingers discovered no injury, and no bear came shuffling behind.

She began to cry. Huge, hacking sobs, torn from her dry throat and depleted body. For the first time in a long time, her tears brought relief.

Thank you, God. I believe.

'What on earth is that?'

I believe!

Tirzah turned to Japheth beneath the coloured hue of a promise and laughed. 'This is Love,' she decided, 'a dog who has earned a name. He saved me from a bear. Love, this smelly man is my husband.'

And far away, on a fragrant mountain beneath the same vibrant, swollen sky, God spoke to another man and said, 'I promise. For all time. Never again.'

A Change of Allegiance

Deborah Henley

When we heard of it, our hearts melted in fear and everyone's courage failed because of you, for the Lord your God is God in heaven above and on the earth below. 'Now then, please swear to me by the Lord that you will show kindness to my family, because I have shown kindness to you. Give me a sure sign that you will spare the lives of my father and mother, my brothers and sisters, and all who belong to them—and that you will save us from death.' 'Our lives for your lives!' the men assured her. 'If you don't tell what we are doing, we will treat you kindly and faithfully when the Lord gives us the land.' – Joshua 2:11-14

25th day of flax cutting

Rahab said…

I'm glad no one will read this, for my quivering hand

struggles to write. The pounding of my heart drowns out the murmuring of the two spies hiding. Spies I am hiding! And I have forsaken my Jericho, to aid the Israelite spies. The spies who look so similar to our people, but have a different culture, history, and religion. I lied to my king, saying they had left the city, while the young men were yet hidden under the bundles of flax on my roof. My roof which is part of the city walls.

When I offered them lodging at my inn, I thought them mere travellers. When I presented my own personal services, they recoiled. It was then that I knew they were no ordinary travellers. If they can afford it, few men refuse a harlot when they're away from their wives.

If I am found out, it will be certain death. But my heart melts knowing the Israelite God dried up the Red Sea for his people to pass through. The same God destroyed Sihon and Og. What hope does Jericho have? What hope does my family have? If such a powerful God wants vengeance on our nation, it will mean certain destruction. I do not want the spies' blood on my hands.

Running my hands over the red mud brick city wall, feeling the strong, rough baked clay, brings no comfort. My fingers circle the rims of the grain jars, but I cannot eat. Even a date has no sweetness now. Even breathing in the warm, nut-laced scent of flax does not settle my lightness of head. The jagged, ochre mountains beyond the city walls, barely lit by the moon, bring tears to my eyes. I have never left these walls, and have never wanted to. I already mourn the loss of my home.

How can an innkeeper like me survive? I must do what I can. First, I need my hands to be still. Perhaps wine will help. Then I will bargain with the spies.

26th day of flax cutting
Rahab said...

The spies have promised kindness, not just to me, but to my family. Despite my profession, they have offered me hope. For saving their lives, they have promised to save mine and any who join me. Clinging to a rope, they climbed out my window, fine dust cascading from the walls. The only noise was the thud of their bodies reaching the ground. They ran into the hills, sprinting with the speed of a falcon.

I replay the oath in my mind, and clutch the only tangible thing from their visit, a scarlet cord. I am to tie the red rope in my window until they return. Under the cover of darkness, I will secure it. Soon it will sit, dangling in the cool night breeze. I must speak to my parents, my brothers, my sisters, and beg them to join me. And I must wait for the Israelite men to return.

I pray to the Israelite God that the spies have returned safely to their camp. I must stay quiet and continue my inn-keeping business, until they reappear. Yet I wake to a drumming heart, dreaming that my change of allegiance has been discovered. Jericho no longer feels like home.

***

2nd day of the barley harvest
Rahab said...

Israel is coming. Rumours have spread of the Jordan River diverting so the Ark of the Covenant could cross. Others living in the wall wail to Yareakh, the moon god. Our people are afraid, yet the words of the men ring in my mind: 'Be strong and courageous. Our God will come with us.' I shall not weep or beg to Yareakh. My hope is in the God who parts rivers. I repeat this promise and it stills my heart. I can return to sleep.

My greatest challenge is to convince my family to come, without telling them why. I made an oath to the spies not to utter their plans to anyone. If I do, our agreement, and my safety, is broken. Will my family trust me? I am to lose my home; I cannot bear to lose them too.

***

14th day of the barley harvest
Rahab said…

Our city is returning to normalcy. Trade is continuing. Israel has not come. I check the horizon every morning and evening. It glows amber during sunrise with the occasional trader visiting Jericho. But of the army, the horizon is bare. My neighbours still pray to the moon god and are praising him for answering their prayers.

My elderly neighbour takes comfort in one of his childhood memories. Forty years ago, the Israelites came. Our forces joined with the Amalekites to drive them out. He believes if the Israelites return our army will prevail.

Have I made the right decision? The scarlet cord continues to hang in the window. I am thankful no-one has questioned me again about the spies or asked about the cord. I try to remember, 'Be strong and courageous. Our God will come with us.'

***

20th day of the barley harvest

Rahab said…

Marching Israelite feet echo from the distance, bouncing on my clay brick walls. I knew they would come! Somehow the scarlet string holds firm despite the foundations shaking. All trade has stopped. Our city gate remains firmly closed. Extra guards are on watch around the streets. With Israel, a strange pillar of smoke or cloud moves through the jagged ochre mountains beyond the city walls. The superstitious believe this to be an omen, although each prediction is different. My family are coming to visit. I hope they will stay.

Earlier today, I kneaded flour and water to make dough. My stomach pounded and twisted just like the mixture. Now the flat bread is baking and the smell twists my stomach tighter. But I need something to feed my family, who will hopefully soon join me. My legs feel heavy, as though stones from the bottom of our city walls are tied to my feet. I keep busy, for when I stop, my hands return to quivering. I must trust in the Israelite God.

My family have seen the pillar of smoke, and I know they fear the Israelite God. Yet they keep their homes and old gods. Trusting in the skulls of our ancestors with shells for eyes. How can something unable to see, see what is happening here?

***

25th day of barley harvest

Rahab said…

For the last few days my morning has begun with men in the watch towers shouting warnings of the approaching Israelites. The sky has become a golden hue as our archers ready themselves, but…

Israel is marching, not attacking. From our walls, the people look down. We watch the golden hue turn to blue. My neighbours continue to call on Yareakh. Some beg for deliverance; others laugh at the Israelites. How can they laugh knowing the stories of the desert invaders' conquests?

The Israelites wear simple linen tunics. Others, simply a skirt. They have not pillaged or paid for their warrior attire. Beards collect dust, brought up from their pounding feet. Leather sandals step, one foot in front of the other. These desert warriors appear ordinary, unthreatening, but we've all heard the stories of their victories.

The Israelites carry an ornate box, which they say is the 'Ark of the Covenant'. The rectangular box is the size of a small man. It flashes in the sun and appears to be gold. Two golden winged creatures sit on its top. Four golden hoops hold long, wooden poles. Men lift the poles to carry the Ark of the Covenant.

Ark means chest, which must refer to the box. Covenant means agreement or pledge. What agreement have the Israelites made with their God? Is it written inside the box? Or do they carry jewels and treasure inside?

Marching armed guards lead the procession. They are followed by marching priests with trumpets made of curved ram's horns and priests carrying the agreement chest. The rest of the army is marching in the rear. They carry sickle-swords, spears, bows, slings, and shields. Yet they do not lift a bow, but rather they parade on. Men of all ages, snaking around our wall quietly and then returning to their camp.

For days Israel has marched around our walls; our walls that no army can breach. The foundations are stone, the height of three men. On top of the stones are our mud brick homes, the height of another four or five men. Our city trusts in the walls for protection. The grain stores are full. Our water spring is inside the city. The king is keeping the city gate shut, and his people and possessions inside the wall. We are prepared for a long siege, as long as it takes. To penetrate the city is impossible. But Israel carries the box which parted the Jordan River: their God is with them.

My family have agreed to stay, though they don't understand why. I am not sure if they're just enjoying the view of the parade below or the food I have stored. We have dates, raisins, onions, beans, lentils, and have been feasting on goat. My nephews are tiring of playing knuckle bones and being cooped up. Sometimes they briefly leave my house, laughing as they run freely through the streets. My hands struggle to complete anything until they return.

When will the Israelite God take action?

***

27th day of barley harvest
Rahab said…

Huddling in my home, I can barely move or eat. Israel marched today, as they have for seven days. But today, shouts and trumpets reverberated in the city in a deafening roar. My ears are still ringing. The walls of my home shake. Everything is collapsing. Dust fills the air, making it impossible to breathe, or see. My family and I tore one of my dresses, placing the linen over our mouths to lessen the coughing. The children wail, unable to be comforted by their mothers. Beyond our house I hear the screams of others. Still they call on their gods, the gods who are crushed by the falling rocks.

Will the Israelite God kill my family too? Will we find refuge with his people, or die today in Jericho? I must huddle with my family. It could be our last time together.

***

Rahab said…

I think it is the time of the pruning.

I must write, so I remember this story and tell all who will listen. The walls crumbled but my house stood. We heard the cracking of the walls, the rumbling of an avalanche of rocks falling. Even with linen rags over our mouths we could barely breathe. Through the dust, we witnessed the tumbling bricks form a ramp for the Israelite army to climb. My home shook, but it stood firm.

While everyone and everything my family had ever known crumbled, we were taken to the Israelite camp, set up outside the city walls. What remained of Jericho was burnt. Ash and smoke filled the air for days. My kinsmen and I will now settle with Israel. Our new nation has not settled in its new land of milk and honey, so we do not yet have a fixed home. But with this nation we feel a sense of belonging, and I trust in their God. I am entering their history, culture, and religion. When fear overtakes me, I remember, 'Be strong and courageous. Our God will come with us.'

City of Bees

D J Blackmore

But you would be fed with the finest of wheat; with honey from the rock I would satisfy you.' – Psalm 81:16

Caleb

Around me is a harp-song of insects. Flowers echo choirs of bees. A peaceful kind of worship beneath the brow of the sun, its hum reaches me. It's holy on the hillside this autumn afternoon, as I listen to hymns from a synagogue without roof or pillars or walls. Winged things talking in tongues of which I can't understand the meaning. Even still, it makes me smile.

I am Caleb, adopted son of Jacob, an orphan given the love of a family. Here is a place of milk and honey. Israel is home to me. We are the people of Nimshi; and this is the City of Bees.

Tel Rehov is named for the broad valley, but above all things it's famous for its honey. We benefit from the industry of insects. It's our greatest commodity. They forage through the seasons unceasingly, while we toil beneath the sun to gather it. Along the trade route by the Way of the Sea, we sell to camel herders and kings. From the Dead Sea to the Red Sea, beyond the Gulf of Aqaba.

I scratch at a sting on the back of my hand. I smell of smoke and honey. Awake with the bees, I go to bed with the sun, my life is shaped by Tel Rehov's apiaries. I blink at the blue of the sky through the half-closed shutters of my eyes. And as I yawn, I imagine the bone-white clouds are a ribcage, expanding with the breath of the wind. Like the heaving chest of the prophet Elijah, taken up in a chariot through the heavens without his cloak. He left *that* with Elisha, the holy man in the house down the hill, so they say. I peer into the unfathomable blue and wonder. Can the bees fly so far away?

'Why is it that you can lie down in the grass while every day I must spin?'

I start up at her words. Deborah flounces into view to drop down beside me. I turn to face her, squinting against the sun. In a handful of years, I have come to know her like family, but she is sister in name only. We love and fight like siblings all the same.

'My work is done for today.'

'My work is never done.' She glances at me petulantly.

'There are three hundred beehives that need tending. I do my share.'

'You are not the only one. Mother and I spin and dye from the time the sun rises. And who would weave shirts for your back if not for me?' She holds up hands stained with woad plant, almost as blue as the sky. My grin erupts into a chuckle. I roll onto my stomach as her sharp finger pokes me.

'You have woven no garment for me *that* colour. I would remember if you had.'

'The seeds you gave me,' she reminds me, aiming a withering look my way.

'Oops,' I chuckle.

She thrusts hands behind her back. 'It's to be put by for when I am married.' She is sour as pomegranate picked too early.

'Take heart, Deborah. With hands like that, you are safe from any man with eyes, it is fair to say.' I jump up, dodging a stinging slap coming my way.

'You will miss all I do for you when I'm gone!'

'And you will wish you still had me to save you the occasional morsels of honeycomb,' I remind her laughingly. If anyone has a taste for honey, it is the blue-handed girl I have lately struggled with my conscience to see as a sister.

'What did you say?'

I walk backwards into a wall. Stop dead at the weight of the overseer. Fat as a toppling pot, a barrel of a man whose greed for food is almost as great as his hunger for unmarried girls like Deborah, they say. I believe it. I have seen the man eat. I bounce back from his bulge. Almost lose my balance as he rights me.

'It was a jest,' I am quick to say.

'Tel Rahov has orders to fill. Accounts to pay. You had better not be plunging a hand into the honey pot.' His stare is hard.

'Of course not.' My face burns hot as altar incense. It's no smokescreen to this ark of an overseer. He has lived long enough not to be fooled so easily. But then every worker doubtless licks his fingers clean when an occasional honeycomb chunk falls, unseen.

26

The man turns to measure Deborah's retreating form as he would a beast for meat. He chews on the fat of his thoughts with a silence that balls my hands to fists. I clamp the hot words that fill my mouth. His interest doesn't sit well with me.

***

Deborah

'Wool cannot be spun with flax,' Mother reminds me.

'Why not?' I want to know.

'Because we do not wear *shatnez*,' she sighs, longsuffering. 'We do not mix wool and linen. You know this, Deborah.' I shrug as she attempts to reeducate me.

'Cain brought God flax seeds from the field. Abel brought him the wool of the sheep, but when Cain killed his brother, it was ordained that the offering of the sinner should not be mixed with the offering of the innocent. Only priests can wear robes of the wool of the sheep woven with linen.'

I look up from considering my blue hands to roll my eyes. 'It seems ridiculous to me.'

'Must you always question everything, daughter? One day you will learn there is wisdom as well as peace in accepting the rules of your parents—the laws of Yahweh.'

Mother takes up a lock of combed wool in her left hand, the drop spindle in her right. It hangs suspended before she flicks the whorl clockwise to spin the yarn tight. She feeds fibres to the twist, and with deft fingers, slowly draws them out to form a yarn smooth and fine and light. Even before the spindle taps the ground, she winds the twisted wool around the weight of the whorl and repeats the process, time after time.

It is music for the eyes—melody without sound. But does she realise another day is passing in the monotonous strum and pluck of those soundless chords from her hands? Cross-legged I yawn. Long curls of wool lay discarded in my lap.

'Oh, I am reminded to take bread to our neighbours across the street. Perhaps you could do it?'

I look up at her, my reverie broken.

'The husband and wife who house the prophet?'

'The very same,' Mother nods.

'The holy man has the eyes of thunder and lightning.' Has she not noticed? 'I could finish combing the wool while you are gone,' I negotiate.

Mother sighs. 'Very well.' She cannot be bothered to press me further but sets down the spindle and gathers flatbread in linen before veiling her hair to disappear from sight.

I rest easy against the mud-brick wall at my back. I don't realise I have been dosing, when a shadow falls across the sun pooling where I sit.

'Shalom,' greets the man in the doorway.

I gather the wool in my skirts as I stand.

'Peace to you,' I answer. 'Ma nishma? My father is not home. My mother has taken a meal to the needy across the street.'

'No, I realise that.' He lets a smile rest on me a long moment. I squint and hold a shading hand to my eyes to see that it is the overseer who recently spoke to Caleb. 'I have come to bring a gift for the house of Jacob,' he explains, and I return the smile he offers.

'How kind.' I step forward as he hands me a jug.

'Syrup for the sweet,' he tells me, 'surplus as a gift for your family. Your father and that orphan boy he feeds at your table are hard workers. Not often enough is good work rewarded.'

I do not like the name he has given Caleb. If not my brother, he is the closest I will ever get. We are family. But there is truth in what the overseer calls him, so I let it slip. Yet Caleb is a boy no longer. Anyone with eyes can see.

The jug is heavy. The terracotta shines with kiln-glaze. It's a master potter's handiwork and I set down the stoppered pot to admire it. The crock, small handle either side, will be treasured long after the contents have given their last drops.

'This is very generous,' I hear myself bluster, but he waves the thanks away.

'Forget it,' he says, before he's gone again.

I taste the honey now he has left, licking sticky fingers. I can already imagine the taste of it spread on the challah at the feast of Yom Kippur. My mouth is a sudden spring, watering. Father has ever been surly where it concerns the overseer. Caleb has learnt the trait. But is it justified? His kind gesture is at odds with their attitude. I wonder at it, honey still sweet upon my tongue.

***

Deborah
'How long will you be gone?' Mother asks. Our father shrugs.

'There is an order of honey as well as some hives to go to Egypt, and there is no one on whom Pharoah is prepared to wait, not even on the famed bees of Tel Rehov.'

'The feast? You will return for that?'

'Have I ever missed your challah at feast time, wife?' he asks. Mother gives him a smile she reserves for him alone. I roll my eyes in Caleb's direction. He returns it with a grin.

'I will happily forgo the fasting to return for the feast,' Caleb offers. Father gives Caleb a level stare.

'Caleb has been asked to come. I would rather it so,' he admits. 'You remember that lions and leopards are always on the prowl, and they prefer meat to honey. Two sets of eyes are better than one,' he hastens to add, 'and yes,' he nods at her look of worry, 'never fear, I will take my staff.'

'Where did this come from?' Caleb runs a hand over the stoppered jug.

'Oh, it is from the overseer,' I tell him happily. Caleb and Father share an astounded look.

'Why, there is more honey than the little black ant could ever dream of,' Caleb teases me. Then more soberly, 'But still, the other day the man threatened me if I so much as brought home the smallest amount.'

He falls silent to contemplate the crock.

'What's buzzing in your head?' I giggle.

'Why such an honour?' Father answers instead. 'I didn't think good deeds came from the man.'

'Time mellows,' Mother reminds Father. 'I am sure the years have changed all of us.'

Father thinks about that a moment. Caleb and I glance at them, but my mother's cryptic words go unremarked and unexplained.

'There is an overabundance?' Caleb frowns.

'Probably an apology for the harsh warning he administered

the other day,' I say.

The pot is finer than any dishes or vessels in our dwelling place. Caleb pours a slow golden trickle onto his pointer finger, before licking it clean with one swipe of his tongue.

'This season's,' he confirms. 'And it has been a good harvest.'

Father and Caleb are gone before first light. It is quiet without Caleb's banter. He's not here for me to scold, and I have no one to tease me. I admit that I miss him already.

***

Caleb

'When the Israelites fled Egypt in the Exodus, it took them forty years to find a land flowing with milk and honey.' Jacob rubs his beard thoughtfully. 'Yet it only takes us seven days by camel to reach the Gulf of Aqaba. *Forty years*,' he repeats, dumfounded for the reason why our forefathers took their sweet time.

'They could have asked someone for directions.' I grin, catching his eye.

'Ha!' Jacob laughs, 'the pridefulness of men. We never ask for directions. You know that. This is why Yahweh chose women to nurture children. Men wage wars while women wait at home, nursing infants. They are strong in ways that are unfathomable to all but the Creator.'

He says, 'Take the queen bee so busy laying eggs, or her many daughters. They wait upon the male drones who do nothing but eat.'

'It is also the females who sting,' I remind him.

'Only for the good of the colony,' he smiles. 'Our cylindrical straw hives with a flight hole at the entrance and a round lidded handle at the back to remove the dripping combs might seem a cunning plan to us. But they are simple vessels housing the architecture of a dynasty of insects whose palaces are a perfection of hexagonal chambers.'

There are a dozen beehives hanging either side of the panniers of some of the camels. Still, this has not been the first sale made to the beekeepers of the Pharoah. With our cargo are jugs of honey and blocks of beeswax. We are a cavalcade bearing liquid gold.

The horsehairs of an Egyptian's wig could not be fixed without it. Then there are uses for wax in things such as writing tablets and casting moulds. The propolis bees use to stop up holes, we take advantage of in medicine and glue. Then there is the nectar of flowers. Bees are the only insect that provide food for mankind.

'The Egyptian king thinks to liken himself to a bee: a sovereign of limitless capabilities. Someone needs to remind the man that the queen is a female,' Jacob mumbles.

'Did you hear the traders we passed saying Pharaoh has shaved off his eyebrows because his cat has died?'

He turns to me and raises his brows as his mouth quirks.

'I did not.'

While our bees aren't given god-like status, we ensure our beehives are shielded from the heat. In split level flooring in the centre of the city, the people of the town are used to the flight path of the insects that pass the market vendors, the dwellings and scores of inhabitants.

In the near distance I spy a jackal and her two pups. They sit overlooking the progress of the convoy beneath, as it travels through the rocky pass, our camel train continuing soft-footed through sandy terrain.

'Did you know that a jackal can mate with a dog or a wolf and produce young?' Jacob asks. I turn to flick a quick glance in his direction.

'Interbreed, you mean?'

'Yes, half jackal, half wolf.'

'A wolf in sheep's clothing,' I muse.

My thoughts turn to my mother and Deborah at home. Women might be the nurturers, but we are the protectors, and yet we aren't there. I think on the gift of the overseer. Wonder how there was so much extra honey that our modest family alone had been given a gift that would earn the smile of a king.

***

Deborah

Our mudbrick dwelling is perched on the rise of the city. I can scale the hill where Caleb likes to stare up at heaven from the flat of his back. The seeds he's gifted me were bartered for with a hungry traveller for some of Mother's best bread. I know a few of the plants are flowering yellow, but it's the young leaves closest to the ground I want. I don't think we will be able to match the last dyebath for colour but we intend to combine both dye lots together before we spin it, so darker and lighter blue will give depth to the sky coloured cloak we have decided upon.

I pass the synagogue, glancing at the sculpture of a seven-branched candle holder or *menora*. It is beautiful. I run my hand along it in wonder at the craftsmanship then walk on.

Beside it is the house of the woman whose son died, before the prophet Elisha breathed life into him again. As I pass the holy man I dip my head. He is a frightening one. It is said when a group of laughing children called the prophet names, he called two she-bears down from the mountains to tear them to pieces.

Still, he does have a bald head—no lie there. It shines an unearthly light. I glance back up to meet his eye. Does he hear my ungracious thoughts? Know that I am defiant and lazy? My heart hammers as I hurry, making for the mount, only stopping when I spy the woad spikes moving in the wind.

I have no need to waste time on the hill. It is not the same without Caleb. And though I will not let him know it when he returns, I miss him with a heartache that sours my mood. It will be some days before he is home. He will be dark as an Ethiopian with two weeks on a camel beneath the sun.

'Daughter of Jacob!'

My head comes up as I spy the overseer at the foot of the rise. Immediately my mind travels to the convoy of camels on their way to the Gulf of Aqaba, so far away. In that moment, I feel strangely alone.

'Shalom,' I pull my veil close as I approach him, unnerved.

'You have been named as a thief,' he tells me.

'What have I stolen?'

'A crock of honey from the prophet that was given him by the king.'

'The jug you gave me?' I am confused. 'It was a gift. You said it yourself.'

'I remember no such thing,' he denies flatly.

'You came to our house only days ago. Surplus, that was the very word you used.'

'I would never give Elisha's crock to anyone but the holy man himself. The city relies on the apiculture of Tel Rehov. Theft of honey is seen in no uncertain light.'

'I am telling the truth. You know this!'

'And who can verify your story?' The overseer steps close to me.

'Why, only you,' I whisper, as a whirlpool of dizzying wings clamour to flee my chest.

The overseer comes nearer still, his eyes holding a nameless meaning that frightens me.

'Your father and the boy are not here to bear witness. I am the only one that can vouch for your innocence.' The barrel of his body contacts mine, his strapping arms winding around me. I am tight in his embrace.

'I have a proposal to make.' His whisper is a sibilant hiss.

In an instant I understand that being innocent means nothing if the overseer gives false witness.

That hunger and desire can mean much the same thing.

***

Caleb

'You know we named Deborah for a bee?'

I turn on the camel to stare at Jacob.

'Often appropriate. But complimentary? I'm not so sure,' I chuckle.

Jacob's laughter is loud. A belly laugh, it rings around us.

'She is sometimes sweet,' he smiles, his look resting long as he considers me.

'When she is not waspish,' I concede, even as a flame creeps up my neck that has nothing to do with the heat of the day. I turn away to stare at the horizon intently.

'She has the look of her mother.' By the warmth of his voice, I understand that this pleases Jacob very much. Then, as if he hears my thoughts, he says, 'She could have been promised to many another young man, but thankfully her parents and mine were of the same mind. I had already decided upon her anyway. There were others who tried to win her. Luckily Yahweh saw things my way.'

'Men like the overseer?' My words are spoken quietly, but when Jacob meets my eyes, I know I have guessed correctly. He gives a single nod. Unease churns my belly.

'And sometimes I wonder if the man has ever forgiven it. He most certainly hasn't forgotten. His position as overseer is the stick with which he beats me. But I have wide shoulders. His authority is no burden to me.'

The turquoise seaport is now at our backs. Long gone is the invigorating salt spray. Now we pass through towering date palms that line cavernous gullies, boulders and rivulets. We rest a while to water the camels at the springs, and when we stop to eat dates, almonds and drink milk from one of the animals, it's warm and frothy.

Heading home for Tel Rehov, no one is happier than me. Camels aren't comfortable. I yearn for home already. I am weak with longing and wishful thinking. An orphan of a household who took me in and fed me. In love with a young woman who will one day be promised to a man that I don't even dare to dream can ever be me.

***

Deborah

He is old enough to be my father. I do not want to be his wife.

The overseer has made it plain that my theft will be forgiven if I promise myself to him.

'I will talk to your father on his return. I am sure that in the end he will understand it is better you are married to me than you risk punishment or forfeit your life. No one steals honey in Tel Rehov. Just as importantly, no one takes from the seer to the king.'

He strides into our dwelling and casts around for the jug, pointing, 'See your yourself. The name inscribed underneath it says Elisha. It is a most uncommon name in these parts, and I know this is not your name. It belongs to the prophet.'

'If you believe I think you can read, you are a bigger fool than me!' I spin to face him.

Mother rests a warning hand on my arm and says reasonably, 'My husband is not home. You must be aware of this. Just as you were aware of the fact that our hut was empty of all save our daughter when you tricked her like this. Is your hunger for vengeance still chomping away that you must take the girl when you could not have the wife?'

I look from mother to the overseer. The smug smile slides from his lips.

'It may as well be me than anyone else,' he shrugs, as though the past has nothing to do with this.

'You never did like to play fair,' Mother notes. 'If you had been a man of integrity, perhaps you might have found a wife long since.'

'Your daughter is as beautiful as the woman who bore her. Nor am I in my dotage. I will have her with child in a year.' It is a promise.

***

Deborah

'We can appeal this!' Caleb insists. He is angrier than I have seen him, hands balled into fists.

'We can pray,' Father says.

'You think that he will enter the synagogue with repentance in his heart and a prayer on his lips? Yom Kippur is a time of atonement to us, but to a man like him?'

'Regardless of what he does, we must do what's right. Remember the scriptures: 'Vengeance is mine, and recompense. Their foot shall slip in *due* time; for the day of their calamity *is* at hand, and the things to come hasten upon them.''

'And the men in the marketplace who have lived more than three score years and ten? The ones who beat their wives and children. Where is justice?' Father puts out a hand and rests it on his shoulder, but Caleb shakes it off to stride from the hut as though our dwelling can't contain his fury.

'We leave it in bigger hands than ours,' Father calls at his back. Caleb remains silent.

'It is time to go to the synagogue for prayers,' Mother sighs, tucking her hair beneath her veil.

I walk outside and turn to consider Caleb. His glance is already upon me. Eyes prickling with the threat of tears, I want to turn into his shoulder as I often have. But we are no longer children. He walks away, shutting me out of the misery he must feel for me.

My mouth grows dry with repetitious prayer in the hope to change my fate. My belly growls with hunger and thirst unanswered. When the shofar blows a trumpet blast to the ear of the heavens, I wonder if Yahweh is listening.

***

Deborah

'What have I done that you are ignoring me? I did nothing that you should make me feel any worse than I do already.'

'It's nothing,' Caleb mumbles.

'Then if what you say is true, why do you not speak?' I whisper, hot tears dripping slowly down my cheeks.

'You're hurting?' he demands. 'You don't know what it's like to be a man, fatherless, homeless, with nothing but dreams.'

'I do not know what you mean.'

'See, that's the problem. You've no idea how I feel. What I want ... What I need ...'

'Then tell me!' I throw down the linen cloth in anger and stamp my foot. When he takes me by the arms his breath is ragged and he is shaking.

'I want to take you for my wife to adorn with the jewels of my love, for my heart is all I own. But I have no prospects, nothing to give. I was an urchin, cast aside. What kind of repayment is it if I ask your father for you to be my bride?'

I am so filled with frustration that his words momentarily pass me by.

'Oh, so you would see me chucked to the overseer as his wife?' I throw the words. I see they sting. I am pulled to him with a groan and a kiss so hard my heart is pounding with something like the music of tabour, harp and song. Then he tears away from me as if he is drowning in honey, silently floundering, breathless with emotion.

It is only then I comprehend the meaning behind Caleb's words. Sinking to the earth, I am shaking, as love courses through me with the venom of bees.

***

Deborah

'Shalom daughter, I am come to the house of Jacob for the feasting.'

I stare at the prophet, wordless. Where were my manners? What has happened to my tongue? I open my mouth, but no sound comes. And the biggest question: where is the honey crock? I dare not glance around me in case his eyes follow mine and light upon it. I sense the fiery eyes of Elisha miss little.

'Shalom,' my father answers for me, bidding the holy man in. I am sure I cannot walk a step without falling down, yet I manage it. I cast my eyes around our dwelling. Still, the soft candlelight keeps our secret in the corner of the room.

'I am told your mother bakes the best challah this side of the Jordan. All it needs is a dribble of honey from the bees of Tel Rehov.'

We stare at one another in silent horror, as though we are cast in bronze. The prophet starts to laugh as tears fall from his eyes. He points. 'Bring out the jug, there in the corner. There's far too much for one old man like me.'

'Rabbi …' Father falters.

'Allow me.' Elisha straightens labouriously as he goes for the crock. 'Let us give thanks to Yahweh for his unfathomable providence.'

We bow our heads in prayer, but Caleb's gaze is locked on mine.

'I am going to Samaria. This is too heavy to carry along with these old bones. I will leave it here. A wedding gift from me.' He sees my terror and rests his gnarled hand on mine. 'Only, you don't want the overseer. I will make sure he understands me before I leave. Never fear. There is another in your future, and it is not him.'

He turns to my father with a chuckle. 'Is it not time to tell this young man he long ago had your blessing?'

Father throws a glance at Caleb sitting in silent torment, eating nothing. I am desperate to take his hands, rescue him from misery. His eyes upon me are deeper than the sea and limitless as the heavens.

Now I know what love looks like, because it wells inside of me.

Father puts a hand on his shoulder, 'My blessing? Son you know you have it.'

'Then now is the time to speak openly.' Elisha's eyes flash merrily in Caleb's direction.

'Will you take me as I am?' He whispers. 'Flawed yet faithful. Inconstant in many things, but never the heart?'

'Well?' The prophet prompts me. 'I think that's a proposal.

41

Will you give yourself to him in love? Grow in obedience with one another? In time tame the rebelliousness of youth?' Elisha's forgiving smile pierces my contrite heart.

'I will.' My eyes have not left Caleb's. His are now filled with light.

'If we are going to feast, we may as well celebrate a wedding. There are laws and rituals, I know this,' he waves the idea aside, 'but since I am the rabbi presiding here, I say we bend them a little. I don't have time to wait for courting. Samaria will doubtless see the end of my earthly journey. There's a chariot in that sky without a passenger, and lately, I have a hankering for heaven.'

Author's Note:

The oldest beehives ever to have been found were discovered in the ancient, ruined city of Tel Rehov, Israel. Three hundred beehives—one hundred complete—were found in the Early Bronze age settlement. The mudbrick walled city was built on a massive, fortified mound.

The Israelite kingdom was a prosperous city of some two thousand people, containing a synagogue and the reputed home of the prophet Elisha. Potsherd fragments were found with his name inscribed beneath it. While not conclusive, the name is very uncommon in the region. Elisha was a native of nearby Abel-Meholah. Biblical history has also him named as the servant of King Jehu, a grandson of the house of Nimshi. A pot bearing the name Nimshi was also found at the site. This fascinating archaeological finding was inspiration for this story.

Changing of Season's Hues

Elaine Hartskeerl

Those who sow with tears will reap with songs of joy. Those who go out weeping, carrying seed to sow, will return with songs of joy, carrying sheaves with them. – Psalm 126:5-6

Mid-summer was a palette of light pastel tints when hot sun paled the blue sky and a haze shimmered over the fields. The barley harvesting had finished at the end of spring and the last of the wheat waved a soft gold in the gentle breeze.

Chloe straightened up and rubbed her mounded belly. The time was close. Soon, soon she would hold in her arms the greatest joy of her life. The water trickled by her feet as she bent to gather the bundle of reeds. These were to make a new mat for the floor. She paused in the cool shade of the wooded stream. She could see the road meandering past her home and her eyes lingered there as they often did, watching for the travellers passing by.

How her life had changed since one particular traveller had first come by and shared their meal. He had since stopped by many times over the years and enjoyed their hospitality. Indeed, she believed him to be a man of God, and had persuaded her husband to build a small room onto their house. It provided a bed and table where he could rest when he stayed.

***

Silas, her husband, was already advanced in years when he had married her, a dependable solid man, a good husband. The last of her father's five daughters, Chloe was betrothed to the neighbouring widower whose first wife had died childless. Year after year, no babies were welcomed to Silas and Chloe's home and life took on a mundane unchanging character, the same routine, day after colourless day. An evenness, a strange balance to her life had developed over time.

Chloe lifted the bundled reeds to her back and began to walk back to her home. In the distance she could see her husband working side by side with the servants harvesting the remaining wheat. Another servant watched over their small flock of sheep. There had been three new lambs born this year, two males and a female. Lambs provided wool for the clothing she would make, and a male lamb for the yearly sacrifice at the temple. The goats supplied them with milk and meat. A donkey was their only form of transport and a useful carrier of goods to and from the market.

***

She recalled, as she trudged along, the day everything began to shift, to 'tilt'. Elisha, the man of God had joined them. After the evening meal Silas went outside to see to the animals. Gehazi, Elisha's servant found Chloe as she tidied up.

'Mistress Chloe, my master wants to see you.' This was not unusual. She enjoyed their conversations, especially about Elisha's God. He frequently shared the scriptures with her. Scriptures like: *The Lord is my shepherd, I lack nothing*, one of many songs that Israel's King David had written. It brought her great comfort. Another was the foundations of the Israelites' faith: *Hear, O Israel: The Lord our God is one. You shall love the Lord your God with all your heart, with all your soul and with all your strength.* She loved and endeavoured to live by these precepts. Now, filled with pleasure, she went to his room.

'My daughter you have gone to undue trouble for us, is there anything I can do for you? Is there an issue of law with the magistrate I can speak to, on your behalf? Or can I speak to the King – intervene on your behalf for something?'

'What ... oh. Why ...?' Chloe stammered in surprise. 'No. There is nothing. All is well.' She frowned. Had the neighbour complained to him?

'Silas did have dispute with the neighbour over a small tract of land on our boundary. I understood though, that they had come to an amicable arrangement. No, Father Elisha, there is nothing troubling us. Besides, we have family close by who can help us should we have need.'

Her heart trembled with an unnamed fear. There was something in the way he observed her, as though he was seeing through to her inmost thoughts.

'No. No, it's too late. Not only am I too old, my husband is…' Her contemplations stopped here, and she thrust them back into forgetfulness. All night long, buried hope wrestled with corralled desire to gain ascendancy in her heart. By dawn's soft light she was able to greet the new day with fortitude.

Elisha was preparing to leave and asked Gehazi his servant 'What do you think I could do for Silas and his wife?'

Gehazi had been watching their hosts. He saw that Silas was old and there were no children, so he expressed these observations to his master.

'Call Mistress Chloe,' he ordered.

When she came, Elisha said to her: 'In twelve months you will hold a son in your arms.'

'No, Father Elisha, do not tease me. I'm too old. We're both too old. It's not possible.'

'Nevertheless,' he promised her, 'this time next year you will have a baby in your arms.' And taking his leave, he set off down the road toward Mt Carmel.

***

Chloe struggled to maintain her composure. For days she went about in a daze, the desire to birth a child, a longing that had lain dormant for so long propelled her into a frenzy of cleaning. Over and over again she repeated, *The Lord is my Shepherd I SHALL NOT WANT*, until a measure of peace reigned in her heart. Nights were the worst. She tossed and turned, tormented by the impossibility of their age. Heights of faith, depths of despair, chased each other through her emotions.

Fixing her mind on her daily chores brought a measure of peace to Chloe. Even so, the man of God's words broke through the dreary routine bringing violent swings of mood. She swayed wildly from fear that it was all foolishness, a dream, to a fledgling hope, a flickering joy and back again.

Such was the conflict of her emotions and her daily attempt to keep them under control that Chloe failed to notice her monthly flow had ceased. One day her servant remarked, as they washed the linen together, 'Mistress, don't you have any other clothes to wash?'

Distracted as she had been she was now mystified as to why Annie should think there was more washing to be done and replied 'No Annie, I'm sure that is all.'

'That's all right, Mistress.' Eyes twinkling, she added, 'It must be good not having all that extra washing to do.' She turned to go and over her shoulder chuckled, 'It will be wonderful to have little feet around this place.'

'What?' Chloe gasped. Annie's statement stopped her short She considered the past months. Why had she not noticed the missing monthly flow? Why had she not seen the changes in her body? She had been too busy fighting her emotions. Her heart swelled with wonderment and joy as realisation dawned.

'Yes, yes, it must be. I am with child,' she whispered, and with a shriek ran out of the house to find Silas. He had gone to market this morning and on return was unloading baskets of leek and corn from the donkey.

'Silas, my husband,' she shouted jubilantly, 'I'm with child.'

Silas's mouth dropped open. 'Are you sure? My dear wife, you're not dreaming are you?'

'Silas, I didn't tell you before because I was afraid. I confess,

I did not believe it could happen. Father Elisha told me last time he was here that I would have a son within the year.' Tears ran down her face despite the joy welling up in her heart.

'When will this be?' Silas asked.

'Around the time of the wheat harvest.'

'Then we need to make preparations,' Silas planned. 'There is much to be done. I will build a crib for him,' and he had a skip in his step as he went back to his work.

***

Ten months had passed since the man of God said, 'This time next year you will hold a son in your arms.' They had been busy months, making clothes for the little one. Silas was so proud to think he was to be, at last, a father. He spent all his spare time during the winter months whittling toys out of wood, making a child size chair for the baby and crafting a crib in between duties on the farm.

Chloe frequently stopped to rub her belly. It was not difficult to sing her praise to Lord as she accomplished her tasks. Scriptures rolled through her mind. One of David's songs she had come to love was: *For you created me in my inmost being. I praise you because I am fearfully and wonderfully made. My frame was not hidden from you when I was made in the secret place. When I was woven together in the depths of the earth your eyes saw my unformed body. All the days ordained for me were written in your book before any of them came to be.*

Chloe sang these to the babe who was growing within her. He was so precious to both her and Silas.

It was the season of harvest and Silas was preoccupied with

reaping the crops. The time was nearing the baby's birth and Chloe had arranged for a local midwife to come and stay with her. All was in readiness.

Her belly tightened. Apprehension skittered across her nerves, then excitement. She stopped. She waited and yes, the tightening came again. The time had come.

***

Autumn came with its constant changes of colour. The reds and golds of dying leaves abounded everywhere. Chloe moved away from the crib where she had settled baby Samuel. New life had brought joy and laughter to their home. Silas had regained a youthful energy despite his grey hair. Chloe knew God had heard the secret longings of her heart. They named him Samuel - *God has heard.*

There was a change in the rhythm of their days. Silas still had the animals to care for. He still needed to prepare the ground for the planting of next season's crops. Even so, this did not stop him from coming inside to gaze at his son. The fulfillment of fatherhood shone on his face.

Autumn's vibrancy faded into winter's greyness. By springtime baby Samuel was crawling. Mostly he stayed close to his mother's side. When he took his first steps, everything changed. The world was before him, ready to be discovered. He watched his mother spinning the wool from the sheep Silas had shorn. He 'helped' his father tend the animals and attempted to milk the goat, squealing with delight when a squirt of milk hit his face.

***

One warm summer day Chloe took Samuel to the stream. He shrieked his pleasure as the water splashed around him and she laughed at his antics. She sighed, knowing that the hour was nearing time to return to the house. Looking up at the road she was surprised to see men approaching. Scooping Samuel into her arms, she hurried to meet them.

'Father Elisha, shalom. How good to see you.'

'Greetings Mistress Chloe. How well you look.'

'Samuel, say shalom. Father Elisha, this is the child the Lord God gave us as you promised he would.' Samuel buried his face in his mother's neck and mumbled 'Shalom.'

'Will you stay and eat with us Father Elisha?'

'I would be delighted to Mistress Chloe, and perhaps Samuel and I can become acquainted.'

It was a joyous meal. Silas embraced Elisha warmly when he came in from the fields. Samuel warmed to the man of God and the little charmer he was, emerged from his shell. Laughter broke out at his antics until bedtime. Prayers were said that brought a quiet peace and Chloe sang a lullaby about the Lord my Shepherd. The next day Elisha continued his journey, calling in from time to time when passing by.

***

Samuel grew, observing all that was happening around him. A small shadow followed Silas as he went about his farm duties. After the first rains he yoked the oxen to pull the small hand plough, tilling the ground in readiness for barley sowing. Samuel played behind him. A mischievous giggle captured Silas's attention. Samuel was about to eat a fat, wriggling worm he had found in the soil.

'Aba he won't stop squirming,' Samuel continued to giggle. Silas gently removed the worm and gave him a handful of seed to sow.

'Throw it over the ground like this son,' and he demonstrated the art of broadcasting the seed.

Another winter came and went. Another spring and summer and with each changing season Samuel learned the way of the land. Early every day his mother taught him to read and write. Then he would join his father on the farm. He was given responsibility for feeding the animals. He learnt to milk the goat. By the time he was seven years old he was required to help with small farm duties.

Summer was in full swing and the last of the wheat harvest underway.

'When you have finished your studies this morning, come and help bring in the sheaves. The servants have started scything the last stands of grain,' Silas said to Samuel on his way out the door.

'Yes, Aba.' Samuel's usual sparkle was absent.

'Are you well my son?' Chloe studied him closely.

'Yes, Ima, but I wanted to go to the stream today.'

Once his lessons were complete however, he went out to join his father gathering in the sheaves. He helped, heaping the stalks of wheat together for one of the servants to bind. Samuel stopped and looked longingly at the shade trees at the edge of the field. He shaded his eyes. Then clutching his head, he staggered.

'My head, my head, Aba my head is hurting.' He fell to the ground.

Silas ran to his son. Samuel was deathly pale and groaning, his brow furrowed with pain. His son needed help. Howbeit rain was expected, rendering it necessary to bring the harvest in. He couldn't stop now.

Calling one of the servants, he ordered, 'Take the boy to his mother,' and anxiously watched them depart.

Chloe looked up from her chores to see the servant carrying her son. She took him, cradling him in her arms. Something was terribly wrong. He appeared to be asleep, yet he groaned.

'Samuel, Samuel, my son. Wake up, wake up.' Fear clutched her heart. 'Please wake up. Oh Lord God, do not desert us now. Help us. We are desperate for your help. Oh Lord God, you gave him to us. Are you going to abandon us now?' She wept as she prayed, realising that the boy's life was ebbing away even as she held him.

What could she do? This was not something she knew about. Was there a poultice she could apply? Where would she place it? He did not seem to have a fever. Perhaps an herbal mixture to drink. But he was too sleepy to swallow.

'Oh God, what shall I do.' She began to recite the Songs of David.

Bless the Lord O my soul and forget not all His benefits. The Lord is my Shepherd, I shall lack nothing…even though I walk through the valley of the shadow of death, I will fear no evil for You are with me.

She stopped as a cry burst from her lips. 'No, no, I won't believe Samuel is….'

Have mercy on me O God for in You my soul takes refuge ....
I am in the midst of lions, among ravenous beasts.

She choked over the words and forced herself to continue.

Be exalted O God above the heavens, let Your glory be over
all the earth. They spread a net for my feet, I was bowed down in
distress.

She took a deep breath.

My heart is steadfast O God, my heart is steadfast... From
everlasting to everlasting, the Lord's love is with those who fear
Him... I will lift my eyes to the hills, - where does my help come
from? My help comes from the Lord the Maker of heaven and earth.

Samuel had stopped breathing. Her tears bathed him as she
carried him to the room set aside for the man of God. Laying
him on the bed she watched him for any change. Perhaps the
power of the man of God was even yet in the room, on his bed.

'If this doesn't help, I will go to him,' she anguished. She
resolved to wait, then changed her mind.

'Annie, please pack a small bag with a change of clothes and
some bread and cheese. I'm going to the man of God.'

With this she went out to find Silas in the fields.

'I am going to Father Elisha.' He lowered his scythe and
studied her.

'Why? Is Samuel all right?'

'All is well. I...I simply need to go to Father Elisha.'

'I'll send a servant to the house with the donkey, and may
the Lord God go with you.'

Chloe saddled the donkey and ordered the servant, 'Lead
on as fast as you can.'

They had more than twenty miles to traverse and it was not

likely they could travel there and back in one day. Nevertheless, she was determined to implore the man of God for help, the only one she knew who could do something... other than the Israelite God of course, and He seemed to have deserted her.

Mile after mile she kept repeating *the Lord is my Shepherd, I shall not want... my heart is steadfast O God, my heart is steadfast.* Before Samuel had come into their lives, the years had been like a summer washed with monotony, without colour, faded. Samuel had arrived like a burst of autumn colour, ever changing. Now the chill of winter had fallen over their lives, a chill that not even the inside warmth of fire side could dispel. The coldness in her heart held the bleakness of a dark winter's night.

Over and over, Chloe repeated. *My heart is steadfast O God, my heart is steadfast.* In truth, her heart was frozen within her. She struggled to keep deep, wrenching sobs from erupting. Through her tears she could see Mt Carmel away in the distance and reminded herself, *I will lift my eyes to the hills, where does my help come from? My help comes from the Lord the Maker of heaven and earth.*

A burst of insight flashed through her spirit. God was the great Creator. Did he not create life? Could he not bring life back to her son? And Chloe recited David's songs with renewed vigour.

***

Elisha was preparing for a round of celebration and sacrifice throughout Israel when he saw in the distance, figures approaching.

Watching, he called Gehazi. 'Is that not Mistress Chloe? She seems to be in a hurry. Go quickly to meet her. Ask her: Is all well with you? Is all well with your husband? Is all well with the child?

Gehazi ran to Chloe. 'All is well,' she said.

Reaching the man of God, she fell at his feet. Gehazi tried to push her away.

'Leave her alone,' said Elisha. 'She is deeply distressed, and the Lord has not shown me why.'

An agonised sob broke from her. 'I didn't ask you for a child. I didn't want you to raise my hopes.'

Elisha's brow furrowed with concentration as he heard Chloe's impassioned cry. 'Gehazi, take my staff. Run as fast as you can. Do not stop for anybody, do not talk to anybody. Lay my staff on the boy's face. Go now.'

Chloe clung to Elisha's feet 'I will not leave you. I need you to come.'

'Very well. I will go with you.'

Gehazi ran on ahead. Elisha and Chloe followed, accompanied by Chloe's resolute muttering, *Though I walk through the valley of shadow of death, I will not fear, for You are with me.*

Chloe rode the donkey and wondered what Elisha might do. How could he possibly change things? She could hope the child was simply deeply asleep, yet she knew in her heart of hearts that life had gone from Samuel's body. What did she expect the man of God to do? The picture of the boy's lifeless body lying on the bed slipped through her mind and tore at her heart, crushing her hope. Once again, she steadfastly began to recite David's songs bringing comfort to her tortured soul.

When they neared her home Gehazi ran out to meet them, his face shadowed and his shoulders stooped with sadness.

'He has not awakened.'

***

Reaching the house Elisha went straight to the room set aside for him, where the boy lay dead.

He shut the door on the two of them and prayed, 'Lord God, you gave this boy to Silas and Chloe. According to your unfailing love and great compassion, have mercy on them and restore his life.'

With this, the man of God lay on the boy, covering Samuel's eyes, mouth, and hands with his own. Minutes passed and slowly warmth returned to the child. Elisha walked up and down the room, thanking God for his goodness, then once again stretched himself over the boy. Samuel sneezed several times and opened his eyes.

***

Chloe paced up and down. Elisha had shut the door. What was happening in there? What if…. What if nothing happened? Oh, she couldn't bear the thought. Up and down, up and down she paced. The nails she never bit were now a sad mess.

She heard Elisha summon his servant. 'Call Mistress Chloe.'

Chloe did not wait to be called. She ran to the room. Samuel was alive and chatting with Father Elisha.

She fell at the man of God's feet, words failing her in her joy at seeing her son well.

'Take him, Mistress Chloe, and may God bless your family. The Lord God, the maker of heaven and earth, gives life. Continue to hold fast to the scriptures. Moses commanded us to love the Lord our God with all our hearts, to listen to Him and hold fast to Him. Life and blessings flow from this to you and your family. Guard your heart, for this is the wellspring of life.' Saying this Elisha departed.

***

For Chloe, the day had taken on a spring-like atmosphere. There was a softness in the air, a gentle waft of warm breeze, as though heaven itself was hugging her. She could hear sweet birdsong. They were rejoicing too, she was sure of it. Her heart sang a song of praise, *The winter is past, the rains are over and gone…the season of singing has come…the blossoming vines spread their fragrance.* New life, resurrected life, brought a different perspective to the future, and taking Samuel by the hand, Chloe went out to join Silas gathering the sheaves.

Yana's Song

Ruth Corbett

*'For I know the plans I have for you,' declares the Lord,
'plans to prosper you and not to harm you, plans to give
you hope and a future.' – Jeremiah 29:11*

Yana[1] sat bolt upright on her mat. Her heart pounded like a battering-ram. The clash of swords, and the screams of her sisters echoed in her mind. Her mother's anguished parting look tore at her heart. She felt once more the burning of the crude rope around her wrists. Despair swirled around her like dust. The dust stirred up by a hundred hooves as her captor carried her further and further away from her home, from Israel.

Sobbing engulfed her: tears splashed down her cheeks, her thin body shook. She'd lost her beloved parents, her brothers and sisters, her town, her country - her freedom. *Why had the Lord let this bad thing happen? He could have stopped it.*

If only she could be held in her mother's arms again. She was eight years of age yet she felt like a little child. She missed her family – how they looked her in the eyes with love. Before she had belonged; now she was merely a possession of her mistress.

She wiped her wet face with her hair, drew the blanket around her and curled up on the woven mat. A still, small voice comforted and calmed her – *I am Father of the fatherless.*[2]

***

'Make sure you knead the dough properly. I don't want to have to do it again myself.' Damali stood for a moment in the doorway with her arms crossed.

Yana gulped and kneaded the bread with all her strength, but her mind strayed away to her family and friends. Had they been crying too?

A tiny sparrow landed on the shelf. 'Shalom,[3] little bird.' Yana kept her voice to a whisper so that Damali wouldn't hear. 'You're up early, like me! Thank you for your song. Will you be my friend?'

The bird's chirping reminded her of a baby sparrow with an injured wing that she and her sisters had nursed back to health. They had taken turns feeding it milk-soaked breadcrumbs, night after night, willing it to live.

'You'll have to learn to work quicker than that. I could have done it in half the time.' Damali drained her fresh vial of verbal venom.

Her footsteps scuffled the ground and the sparrow took flight.

'Now that the sun is up you can fill and trim the lamps.

Make sure you don't spill any oil. After that, sweep the floors.'

Yana swept the courtyard with a heavy heart. Suddenly, a metallic clash in the lane rent the air. She dived for cover, dropping the broom. It knocked over a scent bottle, smashing it into jagged pieces. Damali stormed outside. 'Oh no! Not my grandmother's keepsake! Anything but that! It was priceless.' Her wail was shrill enough for all the neighbours to hear. 'How could you be so clumsy?'

'Forgive me, mistress. The noise sounded like swords.' Yana's face flushed with shame. She began picking up the myriad of fragrant pieces - a picture of her shattered heart.

Remorse at the catastrophe of the broken keepsake ate into her soul until she remembered her father's words when she'd smashed one at home. 'Never mind. It could happen to anyone. People matter more than things. You are more precious to us than a shop full of treasures.'

Hour after hour Yana followed orders. She shut her lips tight, but her frown flashed fury. *I'm only a child. You are expecting me to work like a woman. It's wrong! It's not fair!* Her flaming thoughts burned up more energy than the mountain of tasks.

Damali's words stung like a swarm of wasps.

Doesn't she know how to be kind?

No. You teach her.

Yana's mouth dropped open. *Me? But how?*

Smile. Offer to brush her hair. Sing to her. Work with love in your heart. You will reap what you sow.

YHWH's words filled her mind as Damali led her beyond the city gates of Damascus to gather firewood.

Back at the house, she released her burden of wood, and piled it against a wall. She wiped her dripping forehead. Her mouth felt as dry as chaff and her legs felt as weak as bruised reeds.

'Child, come here. You'd better have something to drink. Don't want you collapsing on me.'

'Thank you, mistress.' Yana smiled, looked up to the heavens and gave thanks in her heart. Never had she been so grateful for a cup of sour milk.

Damali handed her a jar and they set off again, this time for water. Yana gazed at the feathery clouds. *Perhaps Ima[4] is also walking to get water.* She sang in her heart,

> *'The Lord is my strength and song,*
> *And He has become my salvation;*
> *He is my God and I will praise Him;*
> *My father's God, and I will exalt Him.'*[5]

'Don't trip on the loose stones and whatever you do, don't drop the vessel!'

Yana gripped the jar's handle so tightly her fingers cramped.

When she would walk with her father back home, he never missed an opportunity to teach her. His words came back to her now and gave her strength. *'Life is not easy. When you face difficult things, remember the* Lord *Almighty is with you. He always has a good plan. We just have to discover it.*

God will never fail you. Don't be afraid, for He will never leave you. Don't be dismayed; he will help you. He will uphold you with His strong hand. He loves you with an everlasting love.'

By the time they returned, the bread dough had risen.

'When you've baked the bread, we can have something to eat.' Damali took a sip of wine and licked her lips.

The thought of steaming bread from the oven kept Yana going.

***

Naaman steered his army horse into the stables' yard and dismounted, giving it an affectionate pat. A servant came running, took the reins and led it away. No words were exchanged. Naaman detested small talk.

He swaggered down the lane and passers-by stood back to let him pass, nodding their respect. His valiant exploits had spread through town. He screwed up his nose at the putrid piles of rubbish, careful where he put his feet.

Entering his courtyard, he glanced at the little slave girl stirring a pot. The aroma of goat meat and onions wafted through the air, mingling with smoke from the fire. Damali needed another pair of hands. Capturing the child was a good move.

The hint of Damali's perfume tickled his nostrils, enticing him into their living area. Naaman flung open his new royal-blue cloak to display a silk tunic, laced with gold thread.

'Not another outfit!' Damali rolled her eyes.

'The king wanted to show his gratitude for my recent military success. Besides, he likes his army commander to look the best – it reflects on him.'

'He does have good taste. Makes you look even more handsome than ever! Maybe I could become his personal perfumer and *I'd* get a new set of clothes!' Damali liked teasing and Naaman knew he was easy bait.

'You're only sixteen and you've already got more clothes than you know what to do with. Look at them spilling out of the cedar chest!'

Naaman wrapped his muscular arms around Damali's

slender waist and gazed into her sparkling brown eyes. 'All we need now to make our happiness complete is a son.'

'I'd settle for a daughter.' Her voice took on a serious tone. 'Sons get called into the army and live in mortal danger, while their mothers stay at home worrying for weeks.'

'No point in worrying. I would teach him how to survive. And when we are old, he would take care of us and the property, and perpetuate my name.'

After their dinner of spicy stew, wine and a handful of grapes, he climbed the outer stone steps to their flat roof and gazed at the glistening stars. Life was better than he could have imagined. At twenty-four years of age, he had the status of highest-ranking officer, favour with the king, wealth, servants, a beautiful wife, and a lavish home. His future gleamed with potential.

Later, he stretched out with Damali on their bed, and pulled the woollen blanket around them. The flame of their oil lamp flickered – enough light to show his wife's fine features and soft curls. He snuggled closer and drifted off to sleep.

***

Yana had never felt so exhausted. Lying alone on her mat, she ached all over, but the deepest ache was in her heart.

Her father's words echoed back to her. Each evening after their meal he would speak words of blessing from the Torah over their family.

'The LORD bless you and keep you; the LORD make his face shine on you and be gracious to you; the LORD turn his face toward you and give you peace.'[6]

Yana's heart filled with wonder that the LORD would turn his face towards her. She pictured his smile. She prayed for her parents and each of her sisters and brothers until sleep overtook her.

Long before dawn, nightmares of her capture plagued her yet again. Jamming her hands over her ears could not block the screams and the thundering of the horses' hooves replaying in her memory. Her tears cut fresh rivulets down her cheeks.

If only she'd stayed close to her family that day and not strayed away. If only she had helped them haul water from the well and not raced off to explore. A walnut tree beckoned her. She hauled herself higher and higher, snapping off every walnut within reach. She liked giving her family nice surprises. Hugging the trunk, she peered through the branches. In the distance she could see her family coming to find her. 'Ima, I'm up here!' A song of joy stirred in her heart and broke free from her lips.

She clambered to the end of a thin, laden branch and an ominous creak warned her - too late.

She screamed, scrunched her eyes and hurtled through the branches. *This is not going to end well!*

Hands, not the ground, broke her fall. Her relief was short-lived.

'Caught you! Now you are mine!' A foreign voice gloated like a spider with a creature caught in its web. Menacing eyes invaded her soul. The soldier's bronze breastplate sent shivers through her bruised body. He held her under one arm like firewood, restraining her violent squirming and kicking.

'Let me go! Put me down!' Yana's screech bounced off his armour.

'I was wanting a slave for my wife, and you fell into my

arms. Meant to be!'

'I'll tell my dad on you.' Defiance charged her words with fiery force.

His mocking laugh charred her frayed hopes.

A rough hand clamped over her mouth. 'No more shrieking. Understand?' He wielded his sword to enforce the message. 'You should be grateful that I saved you.'

He strode downhill and dumped her in his chariot, tying her wrists tightly. Shoving in between her and his stone-faced shield bearer, he shook the reins. The chariot lurched into life. Yana turned her head in time to see her mother rushing over the brow of the hill, her hands laced over her forehead and her face etched with despair. Her sisters' screams voiced her own forbidden ones. She couldn't even wave goodbye. Tears blurred her vision.

Moments later a band of horsemen met them. They thundered away together, confronting every opposition with the clash of blood-stained swords.

Yana took a deep breath. *I'm not going to relive my capture one more time. I might be a slave on the outside, but inside I choose to be free.*

Dear Father of the fatherless, thank you that you heal the broken-hearted. Please can you find all the broken pieces and fit them together.

I forgive my master for tearing me away from my family. Please help me love my captors.

The Lord's peace enveloped her. Through the latticed window, a feather of moonlight caressed Yana's face. It reflected the glimmer of hope in her heart.

***

Naaman was strapping up his sandals when his world turned upside down. An ominous patch of white skin had appeared on his foot. Dread assailed him like a dagger at his throat.

No! It can't be! How can I have caught leprosy?[7] My life, my dreams for the future will be ruined.

I'll become an outcast…I'll lose my position in the palace and on the battlefield… and in my home. I'll lose all hope of becoming a father. I'll lose Damali. I can't risk infecting her. I couldn't bear the thought of her becoming disfigured.

Perhaps I can hide it – but for how long?

Open sandals couldn't conceal much. He couldn't wear his boots everywhere. If it spread to his hands or face, everyone would see it. How would he live with the shame? He wouldn't wish this affliction on his worst enemy. It was a fate worse than death.

Fear charged through his mind. He thought of the victims he'd seen – their once olive skin bleached white. Pitiful shadows of their former glory - their clothes, good looks and future in tatters. Forced to live outside the city walls, they rasped out, 'Unclean! Unclean!' to warn people to keep their distance to avoid catching the dreaded disease. They reeked of suffering.

His hands grew clammy. Sweat dripped from his brow. He would trade all his gold-threaded garments and stores of silver and gold for good health and time with his family. That was all that mattered.

Lost in his thoughts, he didn't notice his wife slip into the room. She put her arms around him.

'Don't do that!' He pushed her away.

'Whatever's wrong?'

'Nothing. Didn't hear you come in. Just need time alone to think.'

'Alright ... but you don't need to slay me with your words. I'm not your enemy.'

Naaman caught the words muttered under her breath and winced at the hurt on her face as she retreated outside.

He grasped for hope in a sea of despair. *Maybe it's not what I think it is. Perhaps it's something else – some food I ate, or a reaction to a plant that's poisonous. I could be worrying over nothing.*

A plan formulated in his mind. He'd go away on his own for five days and give his skin time to heal.

He paced back and forth, pulled at his hair, punched the mattress with his fists, waiting until Damali and her slave girl had set off for the market. With a shaking hand he wrote a note to her and another to dispatch to the king, explaining that he had an urgent mission to undertake for royal security.

'I don't want to go hungry,' he mumbled as he rummaged in the storeroom, gathering up a water vessel, a goatskin of sour milk, some honey wafers, dates, parched corn and smoked fish. He changed into an old tunic and put on a woollen cloak, sliding his knife into his belt. *I'll need a bird snare, my short sword and my bow and arrows.*

After loading his provisions into his carry bag, he set off down the narrow lane to the stables, cringing whenever he passed someone.

At the city gates the people jostled each other. Beggars squatted in the dust swishing away flies, pedlars displayed their wares, labourers milled around hoping to be hired, children trailed behind their mothers.

Naaman galloped away from them all into the wilderness. Before sunset, he dismounted at a winding river and set up a makeshift shelter with debris from the latest gale.

The days passed with agonizing slowness. He missed Damali's warmth, company, and cooking.

Memories mocked him as he recalled the countless burnt offerings and sacrifices to other gods that he'd made at the Temple of Rimmon with the king. Surely they should count for something… But he'd never heard of those gods healing anyone. They were distant, vindictive, unknowable.

On the fifth day he faced the grim reality – the leprosy had not healed. Instead, it had invaded more of his flesh. He thrashed a tree with a stick and hurled rocks into the river.

***

Naaman approached the throne room in the palace with a churning stomach. The king caught sight of him and ordered his two bodyguards out of the room.

'O king, my humble apologies for my abrupt departure.'

'Naaman, good to see you back. You left me wondering after your message. Did you succeed on your mission? What was the royal security risk?'

'O king, it was me.'

The king's brow furrowed. 'I don't understand. You could never be a traitor. I trust you with my life.'

'Forgive me, but I must relinquish my position as army commander. I do not wish to stop serving you, but how can I continue? I've developed a dreaded skin condition.'

'No! It cannot be true!' The king buried his head in his hands.

Naaman's heart thudded. Would the king dismiss him immediately?

'You are young and fit. I know such conditions are deemed incurable, but miracles do happen. Don't give up hope. You have overcome worse enemies in the past.'

The king clasped his hands. 'I want you to maintain your position. You are too priceless to withdraw. You'll just need to avoid close contact.'

'Thank you!' Naaman bowed low, overwhelmed with gratitude.

He rode home, allowing himself a flicker of hope.

How could he soften the blow? There was no easy way to drop a millstone on Damali's heart. Would she be repulsed?

'Many waters cannot quench love.' It was the last response he expected.

That evening, Naaman retreated to the roof with his bed mat. He caught a glimpse of the slave girl watching him from the shadows, her little brow furrowed.

***

One month later

'What's wrong, Mistress? Why are you crying?' Yana stood at the open doorway.

Damali lay sprawled on her bed, sobbing, gasping for breath, unable to answer.

Yana fidgeted, torn between the yearning to comfort her, and the risk of making her angry. A sparrow in the courtyard burst forth into song. She recalled her father's endearing name for her – *My Little Songster*. Praying for courage, she entered the room.

Resting Damali's lyre in her lap, she began strumming.

'I will sing over you with joy;
I will quiet you with my love.
I will wipe away all your tears;
I will calm your unspoken fears.
When trials come, I'll lead you through,
I will take great delight in you.'

'That's beautiful. I didn't know you could sing.' Damali calmed and sat up, sniffing.

'I sing all the time in my heart. It helps me.'

'Who is the song about?'

'It is about my Heavenly Father. He is Father to the fatherless. He can help you too.'

'I cannot hide the truth any longer. My life is wrecked. My husband has l..l..leprosy.'

'If only my master would see the prophet who is in Samaria! He would cure him ...'[8]

'How can I believe that? Not even doctors can heal leprosy so how could some foreign prophet cure him?'

'Elisha is a man of God, like a commander-in-chief. He listens to God, then speaks out what he hears God saying and miracles happen. Words are powerful – they can bring life or death, healing or hurt.'

Damali rubbed her finger across her lip. 'I do not know your God. What is he like?'

'He created the sun, the moon, the stars, the trees, the

flowers, rain… everything.' Yana spread out her hands and looked at the tiny blue veins. 'He made our bodies, so he knows how to fix them when we get sick. Sometimes he chooses to use a prophet to make us well again.'

'But how can I know your God would even care about someone from another country?'

'He cares about *everyone* because he made us all. He doesn't mind what country we come from. He is kind and loving.'

Damali's face radiated hope. She hugged Yana, for the first time ever. Wiping her tear-stained face with her outer cloak, she headed up the steps to pass on the message to her husband.

Yana knelt to thank her Father, and to pray for her mistress and master.

When Naaman strode down the steps and disappeared along the lane, she knew he had received her words.

***

Dare he hope? Could this slave girl be a messenger from God? If she wasn't, he'd be laughed to scorn if people found out he'd gone all the way to Samaria on the word of an eight-year-old foreign slave girl. Would the king allow him to go?

'I have good news, O king. At least, *promising* news. I have in my household a girl from the land of Israel…' Naaman recounted his story.

'International relations are never simple.' The king stroked his beard. 'The last time you frequented the soil of Israel was to raid it. And now you want to ask the king of Israel for a favour.' He tapped his fingers together.

Naaman held his breath.

'By all means, go.' The king's face broke into a smile. 'I will send a letter to the king of Israel.'

Naaman and his loyal servants left with their chariots and horses loaded with lavish gifts - ten talents of silver, six thousand shekels of gold[9] and ten sets of clothing. If they suffered no skirmishes, storms, or lame horses, they would reach King Jehoram's palace in Samaria[10] within three weeks.

***

Jehoram, the king of Israel, was savouring the new season's grapes, when his bodyguard stirred him back to royal duty.

'O king, forgive me, but you have important visitors. They're laden with gifts and have brought this letter.'

The king unfurled the scroll and read aloud its message. 'With this letter I am sending my servant Naaman to you so that you may cure him of his leprosy.' It was signed by the King of Syria.

The words stung like a scorpion. He threw the scroll across the room, and tore his robes.[11] 'Am I God? Can I kill and bring back to life? Why does this fellow send someone to me to be cured of his leprosy? See how he is trying to pick a quarrel with me!' His roar reverberated through the walls.

Was the king of Syria trying to shipwreck their fragile peace? He paced back and forth. He'd have to stall his guests - anything other than antagonize them. They must be hungry after their arduous journey. Their horses would need watering too. His servants scuttled off at his bidding. He warned them to keep their distance. Leprosy was the last thing he wanted in his palace.

Royal gossip gallops fast, and so King Jehoram was not surprised to soon receive a message from the prophet, Elisha.

'Why have you torn your robes? Have the man come to me and he will know that there is a prophet in Israel.'

***

Naaman's hope rose like yeast in the heat. The prophet had summoned him; he would surely heal him. Naaman's horses and chariots drew up in a flurry of dust at the door of Elisha's house.

But Elisha did not appear. Instead, a messenger conveyed his words, 'Go, wash yourself seven times in the Jordan, and your flesh will be restored and you will be cleansed.'

Naaman exploded with anger. Had he come all this way to be humiliated?

'Where is the prophet?' He spat out the words. 'I thought that he would surely come out to me and stand and call on the name of the LORD his God, wave his hand over the spot and cure me of my leprosy. Are not Abana and Pharpar, the rivers of Damascus, better than all the waters of Israel? Couldn't I wash in them and be cleansed?'

Fury flared in his veins. He leapt into his chariot and left in a rage.

Naaman's servants rode alongside him. 'My father, if the prophet had told you to do some great thing, would you not have done it? How much more, then, when he tells you, "Wash and be cleansed"!'

My father - the words brought him to his senses. His servants cared about him, as did Damali and his master, the king. And even his slave girl! He could not return and tell them he hadn't followed the prophet's instructions. His fury dissipated.

What if the prophet sensed he needed more than skin-deep healing? The thought hit him like a thunderbolt. All his life he'd been trying to prove himself, to win his father's commendation. Status and achievement had become a driving force, goading him on. He wanted to be in the limelight, to be honoured and praised. He'd never cared about who he crushed on the way.

***

Naaman waded into the muddy waters of the Jordan. Part of him screamed, *You're insane! This water couldn't clean anyone, much less a leper!* Yet a still, small voice urged him to release into the current all the inner turmoil he'd been dragging around for years.

Each time he dipped his head under, something sprang to mind - his explosive rage, his seething hatred, his sense of entitlement, his gloating pride, his selfishness, his fear of rejection, his greed. The man of God must have known he needed seven immersions to be free. He emerged from the water the seventh time and his flesh was restored, as clean as that of a young boy.

He looked at his servants, their mouths gaping, their eyes full of wonder.

'Now I know that there is no God in all the world except in Israel.'

***

As the days passed, Yana noticed a change in Damali.

'Yana,' Damali hesitated. 'I see you pray before you eat. Will you pray out loud?'

'I would be very happy to thank God with you and pray again for my master.' Yana beamed.

While they ate Damali asked her about the God of Israel. The more Yana shared, the more her joy bubbled over, and the deeper her love for the LORD grew.

When it was time to sleep, Damali gave her an extra blanket. 'Thank you for your help. What would I do without you? Tomorrow, I would like you to play the lyre and teach me one of your songs about your Heavenly Father.'

'That will be a joy.' Yana lay in bed softly humming a new song.

Damali sang with her, and her face showed a peace Yana had not seen before.

Other surprises came. Damali gave her honey wafers before they set off to gather firewood. 'They'll give you extra strength for the walk.'

Instead of placing the firewood on Yana's back, Damali hoisted it on her own and asked Yana to pick wildflowers. After their meal Damali took Yana to a neighbour's house to meet a young girl. 'You can play together. You need a friend your own age.'

Yana hugged her mistress. 'Thank you!'

The next day Damali was weaving in the courtyard while Yana kneaded the bread. 'Can you tell me more about Elisha?'

'There is much to tell. I'll start with the most exciting story I know.'

At that moment Naaman burst into their courtyard, his face glowing. 'I'm healed, Damali! Yana's God healed me!'

Damali flew into his arms, happy tears streaming down her face. He whirled her around, lifting her off her feet.

Yana slipped inside, knelt down and lifted her hands in praise to God.

Later, as she served their evening meal, Naaman turned to her. 'Yana, thank you for telling Damali about Elisha! If it wasn't for your message, I would still have leprosy, and we'd be facing a life of misery ... Yana, what would make you happiest?'

Yana paused, gazing at the stars. 'I am already happy. But what would make me even happier would be to tell you both more about God's love and power, while I serve you here.'

'You shall have your heart's desire.' Naaman's eyes shone with a new warmth. 'We will gladly listen. You are God's little messenger sent to us ... But maybe not just us ... to our neighbours, our friends, even the king. When people hear how God healed me, they will want to know more about him too.'

'Thank you! The LORD had a good plan after all. I only had to discover it. He wants me to do what I love doing most of all – telling others about how good He is.'

***

Before sleep enveloped Yana, a melody put wings to her words:

> *'LORD, You give me songs in the night*
> *Songs of comfort, spreading Your peace*
> *Songs of healing, songs of Your love,*
> *Faithful love that never will cease.'*

Endnotes:

1   Yana means 'God is gracious' and 'He answers.'
2   See Psalm 68:5
3   Jewish greeting that means peace
4   Hebrew for mum
5   From the Song of Moses - Exodus 15:2 (NKJV)
6   Numbers 6: 24-26 (NIV)
7   Leprosy in Old Testament times was a serious skin disease or skin infection, different from modern leprosy, which is a disease of the nerves.
8   2 Kings 5 (NIV)
9   340.19 kgs of silver; 68.03 kgs of gold
10 A journey of about 316 kms
11 In certain ancient cultures, people ripped apart their clothes to express strong emotion such as shame, anger, or mourning.

The Gift

Wendy Adams

For to us a child is born, to us a son is given, and the government will be on his shoulders. And he will be called Wonderful Counselor, Mighty God, Everlasting Father, Prince of Peace. – Isaiah 9:6

Father has finally decided. Mara is to watch over the sheep. After all, it's the task trusted to the youngest child. Why should it matter that she is not a boy? But Mara knows there is only one reason he has given her this chance. Her brother is ill– desert fever, they say. She shrugs. She loves Eitan, but this is her chance. Her brother will heal, and by then, she will have proven that she isn't too small or too weak to be a shepherd.

Mara creeps into her brother's room. The air is warm and stuffy and she hears laboured breathing—too soft for a snore.

'Do you have any words for me, Eitan? I am to tend the sheep.'

Her brother gives a low groan and rolls over on his narrow bed. 'Leave me be. Or better still, bring me water.'

'But the sheep, Eitan?'

Her brother burrows under his thin blanket so that his words are muffled.

'What?'

'Look out for the wolf,' he says at last. 'Now, fetch me some water. Please, Mara.'

The wolf? He didn't mean it. Nobody had mentioned anything about a wolf. She swallows hard to keep her stomach from jumping out of her throat. She had seen a wolf once–a wild, rangy creature–hunger on legs. It had attacked the flock in a flurry of violence and only her father's staff and the courage of their old, faithful dog had saved them. But that had been years ago. Their dog was long gone and there was no money to replace him with another. Surely, she would have heard…?

Eitan forgotten, she hurries outside to cast her eye over the flock as if a pack of wolves lies in wait at this very moment. But the gentle animals are at peace, nosing the dry soil in search of any tiny remnants of greenery. The wind blows and the dust swirls and plays around her, stinging and blinding. When she completes her tasks, she will take the sheep, her family's only wealth, up Mount Elo, where they hope some grasses remain before the icy grip of winter squeezes the land. She'll guard them all day and night and bring them home, safe and healthy.

She brushes the dust from her eyes with a corner of her tunic and stares up at the mountain. Small to many, but mighty to her. She has longed for this day, thinking it would never come. Her chance to prove that a girl can be trusted to be a shepherd.

In no time, her tasks are done and her mother pushes a leather bag into her hand. It contains a hunk of brown bread, some cheese made from sheep's milk and a flagon of water. Her father gives her his old crook, cut down to size. The sight of it brings pin prickles of tears to her eyes. And Eitan has contributed his first reed pipe. Now it's hers. She breathes into the instrument and smiles. The sound is like a summer breeze on a winter's day. She places it gently into her pocket.

She hugs her father and then kisses her mother's cheek.

'Keep safe, Mara,' her mother says.

'Look after the sheep,' her father says.

Now the time has come and Mara feels a flicker of unease. It's really happening, and the family's future rests on her thin shoulders. This has been her dream for so long, but what if she fails? What if she brings disaster to her family's door? And the wolf. Was there really a wolf lying in wait for them at the top of Mount Elo, or was it just Eitan's teasing?

'Papa, the w…,' she begins, but the sheep interrupt her, bleating in their impatience to be gone.

'They are calling you Mara,' her father says, and he smiles at her. 'My brave and clever daughter.'

She bites back the words and stands tall.

She turns to wave to her parents until the distance swallows them, and Mara is alone with the sheep and the mountain. The sun makes its slow journey across the sky, but it still holds some comforting warmth for this time of year. The sheep know exactly where to go, and Mara is happy following their woolly behinds. Nothing spoils the quietness. She loves to listen to the gentle bleating of the sheep and the sound of their hooves as they strike the stony ground. But suddenly another noise twirls in the air. Mara stops and listens. It's a melody on the wind, a song so sweet it hurts her heart to hear it. But as she tries to capture the sound, it fades away out of reach. Mara shrugs and moves on.

She breathes deeply, letting the fragrant air fill her lungs. Rosemary, lavender, and thyme. And the warm, familiar scent of the sheep. How she loves this land, its dusty plains, and its blue-green hills.

Her legs are strong and the air is intoxicating, so she feels some regret when they finally reach their destination. On the side of the mountain lies food for the sheep and beyond that, a small rocky fold which her father and Eitan had built last summer. It is a shelter for her and for the sheep too if a storm brews. Mara stretches her neck to scan the cloudless sky. No storms on the horizon and she gives a sigh of relief.

The sheep scatter across the field, and Mara feels a moment of pride. She has done it. All sheep accounted for. Her only company here on the mountain top. A new experience for her. To be alone. She takes out the reed pipe and practises creating tunes. She tries to capture the music she had heard earlier. But it's impossible. Reluctantly, she replaces the pipe and settles down on a patch of soft grass. The sun's journey will end abruptly at this time of the year, so Mara closes her eyes, stretches out and embraces the last rays. She awakes as the sun descends, painting the sky brilliant shades of pink and orange. Soon, the darkness will envelop them. Mara jumps to her feet, and, by the fading light, she sees the huddled shapes of her resting sheep. Mara's stomach growls with hunger, but she knows she must tend to them before she can think of her own needs. She wanders over to the flock. Here is Two-lambs, Stripy, Grey-ears, Old-girl, Sandy-feet … She ticks them off one by one, accounting for them all except for one … Lucky.

Mara groans. Lucky! Why hadn't she thought of keeping her close? Lucky is trouble. If a sheep is going to have a difficult labour, it will be Lucky. If a sheep is going to over-eat on rich, green grass and have stomach bloat, it will be Lucky. If a sheep is going to go missing on Mara's first night of shepherding, it will be Lucky. Mara sighs and thinks it might have been better for her if she had left Lucky at home.

There is nothing for it. She must go find her. Mara looks over at the other sheep. Her heart fills with love for them. They are more than just her family's wealth. They are family too. She couldn't bear it if anything happened to them. Now, she must leave them unprotected, alone. Her heart thumps heavily in her chest. And what if her brother isn't lying? What if a wolf lurks hidden in this lonely place? Should she stay and leave Lucky to her fate instead? It's an impossible decision. A loud bleating from below shatters the silent night. And at this moment, the darkness falls.

Without thinking, Mara runs, her feet sure and swift on the path that leads down the mountain, the light of the moon and the stars guiding her way.

'Lucky!' she calls. Silence. She stops, her breath loud in the still night air. Nothing. She has lost her.

She cradles her head in her clasped hands and pushes her face heavenwards. The tears fall, the stars her silent witnesses. Through blurry eyes, she notices that one star appears so much larger and more dazzling than the others. She wipes away the tears, clearing her vision. This star is strange, spreading its light far and wide, tingeing the dark night, golden. Mara gasps. Even the other stars blaze more fiercely on this dark night.

And she hears it again. The music of the heavens and the mighty star calling her, urging her onwards. Wonder fills her heart, all thought of the sheep and wolves gone. Her feet move forward.

She walks many miles that night across the mountain of Elo, into the neighbouring valleys, almost to the town of Bethlehem. And there, above a stable outside the city gates, the star comes to rest.

Mara creeps closer, her eyes wide. A figure hovers before the simple wooden structure with golden eyes and wings as white as the flower her mother calls 'the star'. Fear grips her heart, and her breath freezes in her throat. She trembles and her eyes fall away. It's as if she can't hold the sight of this creature in her imperfect mind. And that's how she notices them. Standing beyond the angel and closer to the manger are shepherds just like her. And animals too—donkeys, sheep… and her heart skips a beat. One small, brown half-grown lamb. Lucky! How is it she is here, nosing her way towards the manger? Mara stares, her eyes wide. A man and woman hold a new-born babe, their faces filled with joyous wonder. They have eyes only for the child who seems to be bathed in light from the glorious star itself. They don't see her.

Mara creeps closer still. The baby. What child is this, born in a manger and tended by angels and shepherds alike? His face bathed in the mysterious light beguiles her. He turns to her as if he sees her, but he is newly born and that isn't possible, is it? She can't turn away. She creeps closer until, with one hand resting on Lucky's head, she peers at the baby. And this time there is no question. He looks straight at her and smiles, and in that moment,

Mara gasps. A strange shiver spreads through her body from head to toe. It's as if in that one glance, she and the entire world have been washed clean. Mara smiles, and the baby's mother laughs.

'You have come far on this night,' she says. 'What brings you here, child?'

Mara swallows hard. She is suddenly conscious of her grubby clothes and the dirt under her fingernails. Her hair is a bird's nest. She quickly pulls back from the baby, feeling unworthy. But the woman continues to smile at her. And there is no reproach in the father's eyes. Instead, here in this stable, she feels like she, too, is bathed in the star's glorious light. As if she, too, is someone important, worthy.

'The star led me here, but I was really looking for Lucky,' the words tumble out, 'and my brother is sick, and I think there might be a wolf and I've left all my sheep…'

The baby gurgles and reaches out for Mara's hand. The shock of his touch is electric. It's like being warmed by the fire after a bitterly cold day. She feels both the heat and the pain. It's like being seen for the first time, really seen and having no place to hide the good or the bad - everything found in a human heart. Mara feels all things, as her life story plays before her eyes - the blessings… the hardships… sadness and the many joys. All the shapes and patterns that make for a long life, a varied life and, in the end, a most satisfying one. And something else. Something she doesn't understand. Something greater than all these things. A connection, a bond that stretches from heart to heart, from life to life, from her moment in time across all time. She breathes it all in and then lets it go.

'Who are you?' she whispers, and she notices for the first

time the gifts that have been left for the baby. A loaf of bread, brown and oaty, a handful of olives, green as precious stones, and a wedge of cheese golden as the sun. She bows her head. What is left for her to give?

She strokes Lucky's head and gently rubs her silky ears. She looks into the sheep's dark eyes, seeing herself reflected in her pupils. She asks and finds the answer in those bright orbs.

'For the baby,' she says. Her throat tightens as she nudges the sheep forward.

The baby smiles again, and his parents thank her. A boy with a drum plays a song for them and the shepherds bow their heads.

For a moment Mara's heart fills with sadness for the loss of Lucky and she wonders how she'll explain it to her parents and Eitan. Would they think she had failed after all her boasting that she could care for the sheep? The thought makes her sad, but when she tells this story, she hopes they will understand. She turns and takes one last look at the scene in the stable–an angel amidst shepherds and the mystifying baby being placed in the manger by his mother. Lucky keeps watch. And like the stars and the golden moon in the heavens above, she has witnessed it all. With her very own eyes, she has seen miracles this night. A wolf howls in the distance and his mate calls back, but Mara is not afraid. She knows deep in her heart that her sheep are safe. She knows that on this night, this night of peace, no evil will befall her or her flock. And with her mind filled with wonder for this child who will become the King of Kings, she turns away. The heavenly chorus fills the air with music so sweet it brings tears to her eyes. And like the melody that soars in the still night air, Mara feels that she too is lifted above it all to dance amongst the stars.

A Refuge for Yitzhak

Amanda Deed

The Lord is my rock, my fortress and my deliverer; my God is my rock, in whom I take refuge, my shield and the horn of my salvation, my stronghold. – Psalm 18:2

'No, no, no, Shai!' I scrambled down the steep incline to my cousin's motionless body. One moment we'd been laughing and sword-fighting with sticks – me ready to gloat over my victorious thrust – the next moment Shai gasped as he lost his footing on the loose rock. I watched in horror as he tumbled down the hill. A distinct 'crack' echoed my shout after him, but whether it was a tree branch snapping beneath his falling body, or one of Shai's bones, I could not tell.

When I reached Shai and shook his shoulder, my cousin still did not move, or even wake up. My mind whirled in panic and my stomach joined in. 'Shai!' I called over and over, in an attempt to rouse him. I didn't know what else to do. I put my hands under his arms and tried to drag him back up to the track, to no avail. He was almost the same size as me. I tasted bile on my tongue.

There was nothing for it. 'Don't worry Shai, I'll go and get help.' I stroked my cousin's pale cheek and descended Tel Zorah as fast as I could, though my lungs burned with the effort. Uncle Dotan would know what to do. I hoped. The image of Shai falling down the precipice replayed in my mind all the way down, the sick feeling in my stomach increasing all the way. 'Please God, let him be all right.'

***

'We were just exploring up on Tel Zorah, near Samson's tomb, as we always do. We were pretending to be Samson fighting the Philistines, and he just fell.'

It was hard to keep up with Uncle Dotan and his friends as they raced back up the mount. Dotan wore a frown that told me I was in big trouble, no matter what the outcome was. My heart pounded, partly from the exertion, partly from distress. The journey down to Uncle Dotan's house had seemed to take an age, but the return seemed even longer.

As we finally neared the spot, I pointed. 'There, Uncle.'

I lingered back, too afraid to look, fearing the worst. 'Is he all right?' My voice sounded weak and pathetic. I thought I had grown stronger with sixteen years behind me, but I was useless, as weak as a child.

I saw Uncle Dotan's shoulders slump, and his friends

shook their heads. A sick feeling of dread swept over me in that moment. It couldn't be. It just couldn't. Shai was so full of life – just an hour ago. Laughing. Jumping. Teasing. How could it end with the slip of a foot? I shook my head, trying to clear my thoughts, trying to make sense.

I raised my eyes to see Uncle Dotan surging toward me, his fists clenched, eyes bulging with rage. 'This is your doing! You killed him!' he roared. Never have I felt words sear me as those did. Like a hot knife plunging deep into my heart. He blamed me. It was my fault.

***

The world froze. Time halted. My breath ceased. But my ears echoed with Dotan's screams. The image of Shai's lifeless body being lifted from the ground etched itself into my memory, never to be erased.

With a gasp, my surroundings became real again, and the trembling began. First my hands, then my knees and then my whole body. But there was no time to recover. Uncle Dotan was still charging at me with vengeful fury written on his face.

I don't know how I got my legs to comply, but I turned and ran. Haltingly, wobbly at first, but with the fuel of fear, my strides strengthened and I sped away from my uncle, his friends, and my dead cousin.

Dead cousin.

Shai was my best friend. We'd grown up together. Played together. Laughed together. Even cried together when his mother died. She was my aunt. My mother's sister. She had a terrible sickness that took her swiftly, despite the prayers of the priests and all of us. And now Shai.

***

One look at my tear-stained face as I burst in the door, and Ima dropped the dough she was kneading, wiped her hands and hurried over to me. 'What is it, Yitzhak? Where is your father? Has something happened to him?' Her eyes darted to the door and back as though she expected him to follow me into the room.

I shook my head. If only I had been in the fields with Abba. None of this would have happened.

'Then what, my love?' The concern in her eyes worked like a door-latch being lifted. The whole story of what happened with Shai gushed out between sobs and gasping breaths. I don't know how I even made any sense to her.

But I do know that the word 'dead' got through loud and clear. Her face paled. Even her lips changed from full and warm red to thin and grey. She turned away from me in a rush and vomited into a pail containing vegetable scraps that she would usually feed to the fowl. Strange, the things you notice in the midst of deep distress.

'We were just playing Ima, I swear it. It was an accident. But Uncle blames me. He is coming after me.' I pleaded, desperate, clinging to the sleeve of her mantle. Did she believe me? Shai was her deceased sister's son after all. The last reminder of her gone with him.

'My son, my son, my son.' Tears welled in her eyes as she gripped my shoulders. I could see a thousand thoughts racing through them. Perhaps she looked into my future, our future, as only mothers can do, reading consequences and possibilities, both good and bad. She pulled me into a strong embrace then, as if she could still my quaking body. 'Peace. Be still. The Lord is good,' though her voice did not carry the surety of the words. I detected deep sorrow within her.

Abruptly, she backed away from me and grabbed a hessian bag from a hook on the wall and began to thrust figs, olives, dates and even a couple loaves of bread into it.

'What are you doing, Ima?' It seemed strange to me, that instead of comforting me, she prepared food.

She handed me a jar of water. 'Drink deeply, Yitzhak.'

When I did not take the jar at first, she pushed it emphatically toward me. 'Drink.'

I took it, but still asked 'Why?'

'You have a long journey ahead of you and you will need it.'

Hesitantly, I tipped the jar and sipped. What journey? Ima motioned with her hand for me to keep drinking. So, complying finally, I emptied the jar.

She put the jar on the table then clasped my head in her hands. 'Listen to me, Yitzhak.'

She pinned me with a serious gaze and dread pooled in my stomach again. I whimpered.

'You must go to Hebron. Now.'

'Hebron?' That was miles away – a full day's walk.

'It is a city of refuge. You will be safe there.'

'Am I not safe here?' Alarm filled me.

Ima sighed deeply and sniffed away her tears with a deep breath. 'Your uncle has not recovered from Rivka's death.

Losing Shai on top of that, well, I doubt he will be rational or reasonable. He will come after you, of that, I am sure. He always had a temper.'

'But, can not you and Abba protect me?' I am sure my eyes were wide with panic.

'Perhaps,' she sighed again. 'But I will not take that risk.' Her strength crumbled and she wept. 'I cannot lose you too.' She pulled me in for another embrace, then kissed my damp cheeks, our tears mingling together.

As she wiped my face with the length of her head covering, there came a thump on the door along with a shout. Dotan was there.

Both of us gasped with fright. But, while my legs transfixed to the floor, Ima snapped into action. She grabbed the bag and shoved it into my hands. 'You must go now, Yitzhak.'

She pushed me toward the window on the opposite side of the house.

'Tovah! Bring out that murderous son of yours!'

If anything could motivate me to run, that was it. I clambered through the window.

'Yitzhak,' Ima whispered, pulling my head to her to kiss me one last time.

'One thing, Ima ...'

'Tovah!' Dotan's fists slammed into the door again. He would break it down in a moment.

'Do you believe me?' I asked, choking up.

She nodded without hesitation. 'Run, Yitzhak. Run!' She pushed me away from the window. 'We will come to you as soon as we can.'

***

So, I ran.

I ran and ran.

With an angry Uncle Dotan on my heels, whether real or imagined. I refused to look over my shoulder to find out.

Instinctively I stayed away from the roads and ran directly through the fields to the south where I could follow the valley floor. My legs burned. My lungs burned. But I found energy in sheer terror. My mind played images of my uncle catching me, pounding me with his fists, screaming at me, before breaking my neck or some similar fate. I imagined my poor mother receiving like treatment when she refused to give me up. Or would she?

Crying, coughing, I ran until I fell beneath the shade of an old oak, gasping for breath. And parched. But I had no water. I lay there for a long moment until my breaths slowed, though my heart still raced. Finally, I dared to look back. If my uncle was there, I couldn't see him. But, how would I make it all the way to Hebron without him catching me? I could not continue running.

I turned to raise myself again and came face to face with a viper. Slithering toward me. I froze. Forget Hebron, I wouldn't make it past this moment. I probably deserved it. Perhaps God was meting out judgement even now. It was a small mercy. I supposed I'd rather die by snake bite, than the hand of my uncle.

My breath stuck in my throat. My fingers and toes cramped as I crouched motionless. A bead of sweat rolled down my nose, tickling, begging to be wiped away. But I refused.

It seemed an age, but the viper eventually slithered away and I collapsed onto the ground once more. I would never survive.

***

It seemed only minutes later, the distant sound of voices drifted to me from the track somewhere behind me. I immediately darted for cover amongst some brush, hoping I had not been seen. A futile hope. Surely it would be Dotan. My limbs shook as I waited there, hunkering in the bushes, pressed into them as much as I could, though the branches scratched.

I spied my uncle pass by on the road and what little hope that remained sank beneath the waves of my fear. He had two, no three, friends with him and they all carried thick pieces of wood ready to beat me. I held my breath again until long after they were out of ear shot. Then I slunk out of my hiding space and dragged my feet forward.

What now? Dotan was ahead of me, so I could no longer run to reach Hebron before him. If he turned back, he would surely catch me. If I turned back, I would never have the refuge of the city. But how could I reach Hebron alive with my uncle between me and the city gates?

At a loss, I trudged on, slowly and keeping close to the trees, my mind a whirl of doubt, panic, guilt and pain. Was there even any point? I stopped and sank beneath the shade of a large tree. I took a loaf of bread from the bag Ima had given me and chewed, the crumbs sticking to my dry mouth. Without water, I had nothing with which to wash it down. I tried a fig, but it helped little. The lump of emotion in my throat made it difficult to swallow anything. For the umpteenth time that day, I cried.

***

A foot nudged me out of my hapless stupor.

With my whole body tense, I raised my gaze from dusty sandals, to knobbly knees, to sun-weathered arms, all the while certain this would be my end. Certain that I would look into the face of Uncle Dotan, I clenched my teeth and held my breath. The sun behind the figure made it difficult to make out his features, but this was not my uncle, nor anyone else I knew. Still, I pressed myself back against the tree, cowering.

'Fear not, young man. I'll not harm you.'

I shaded my eyes to get a better look, not ready to believe the man. Yet his face seemed kind, his eyes crinkling at the corners as one who smiled often.

'I am Micah.'

I scrambled to my feet, still clinging to the tree for comfort, though I knew not what help a tree could offer me if it came to it. I nodded, but could not find my voice.

'Where are you headed this fine day?'

Did I dare tell him? I glanced to the left and right along the road. There was no-one in sight to lend aid. I clutched my bag tight to my chest and studied Micah again. If I ran, would I be fast enough? He was not a big, burly man like Dotan, but he might be wiry and quick. I gulped.

Perhaps Micah noticed my discomfort. He spoke again. 'I am on my way to Jerusalem. I have a message for the people there.'

I opened and closed my mouth but nothing came out. I was still in two minds. Run away, or stay and converse with this man.

'Well, I suppose I'll be on my way,' Micah said with a shrug, and he strolled away.

In that moment, I realised he truly meant me no harm.

And upon that revelation, I also realised he could be a help. I pushed away from the tree and hurried after him.

'I am going to Hebron.'

He looked over his shoulder without the slightest surprise in his expression. Like he knew I'd follow him. He continued to walk, so I fell into step beside him.

'It is a pleasure to meet you, young Hebronite.' He handed me a skin of water.

I gave a half laugh. 'I am not from Hebron. And my name is Yitzhak.' I thanked him for the water and drank deeply, handing the skin back to him.

'What takes you to Hebron, then?'

My stomach churned as everything flooded back into my mind. I was too ashamed to tell him the story, but what reason could I give? I was still busy trying to fabricate a story when he spoke again.

'Hebron is a city of refuge.'

At this, I stopped in my tracks. How could he know why I was on this road? Tears welled in my eyes again as he turned to look at me.

'Tell me, Yitzhak. What has happened?' There was no condemnation in his face, only kindness and compassion. And so, right there in the middle of the road, I blurted out the whole story to him.

***

'I didn't mean for him to be hurt,' I cried. 'Shai was my best friend as well as my cousin. But it is my fault he is dead.'

Micah put a hand on my back, indicating we should continue walking. 'Why would you think an accident is your fault? You said yourself that Shai slipped and lost his footing.'

I pressed my lips together. The truth needed to be told. I needed to confess, but shame clamped my heart. I took a deep breath. 'We should never have been there.'

'Oh.' Micah seemed to understand, and yet he didn't condemn me.

'I was supposed to be helping Abba in the fields. Instead, I snuck out with Shai up to Tel Zorah to explore. If I had not disobeyed my father, Shai would not be dead.'

I let the words hang in the air, like thick clouds of fog, heavy with flooding rain. I deserved for my uncle to catch me and kill me. I might as well have pushed Shai down that hill for all the difference it made.

We walked in silence, the gravity of my confession hanging between us. Micah would likely deliver me into the hands of my uncle without hesitation now that he knew I was indeed a murderer. But, he surprised me again.

'The LORD *is compassionate and gracious, slow to anger, abounding in love.*

He will not always accuse, nor will he harbor his anger forever; he does not treat us as our sins deserve or repay us according to our iniquities.

For as high as the heavens are above the earth, so great is his love for those who fear him; as far as the east is from the west, so far has he removed our transgressions from us.

'King David sung these words. He understood something that many of us fail to.'

I looked at him. 'What is that?'

'While here on earth, mankind hold sins against each other, punish each other, take revenge on one another, the Lord in heaven is different. He has open hands and is ready to forgive. All we must do is confess our sins and ask him.'

'But the law says Dotan is justified if he kills me outside the city of refuge.' I said, remembering my studies of the Torah.

'Yes, but the Lord provided cities of refuge as a symbol of the shelter he himself provides.

'If you say, 'The LORD is my refuge,' and you make the Most High your dwelling, no harm will overtake you, no disaster will come near your tent.'

'Besides, your uncle cannot kill you for the sin of disobedience, and that is truly all you are guilty of. Your trial will reveal the truth.' Micah sounded so confident.

I shook my head. 'But I will never reach Hebron. Dotan and his friends are already ahead of me and will no doubt intercept me before I arrive.' I shivered down to my toes, remembering the look on his face as he accused me.

Micah stopped walking and turned to me, placing his hands on my shoulders. 'I shall make sure you arrive safely.'

I grimaced at him. 'I thought you were going to Jerusalem.'

He patted me on the back and continued to walk. 'Jerusalem can wait a few more hours. Your life is more important.'

***

We walked in companionable silence for a long time. We saw no other travellers on our journey. When we reached the crossroads that would have taken him to Jerusalem, true to his word, he stayed with me rather than heading north. Ahead of us, we had the mountain to climb before we reached Hebron.

As the track ascended steeply before us, my thoughts drifted to my mother, my father, my sisters and all my cousins. My heart sank as I pictured their faces and remembered times of laughter and fun with them.

'I will never see them again.'

'Who is that?'

'My family.' I let out a long breath. 'Is it not true that even if I am found not to be guilty of Shai's murder, even if they rule it was an accident, I must remain in Hebron until the High Priest, Azariah, dies? If I am found outside the gates, my uncle may still take my life as the avenger of blood?'

Micah nodded sagely. 'True. Your life is changing completely, and the Lord only knows for how long. But I am sure your parents will come to visit you. They are still free to come and go. Besides, things can change in an instant as you have seen today. Who knows what might be around the corner?'

'What do you mean?' I frowned.

'Azariah may perish next week,' he shrugged. 'Who is to know?'

My eyes widened. 'Or Messiah might come!'

Micah chuckled and nodded, although there was a sadness to his eyes. 'Perhaps.' He shifted the weight of his sack, seeming uncomfortable. 'Though I feel much hardship is to come before that great day.'

'Hardship?'

'War. For example.' He was hesitant with his words, perhaps deciding whether he should speak at all. In the end, he did. 'The people are not yet ready for Messiah. We do not live according to his wishes. We do not truly love him, though we say we do. How does one profess to love and serve and all-loving, all-forgiving God, and then go about cheating their neighbours, leaving the poor to starve, dishonouring the elderly and widows?' He shook his head. 'No, the Lord has pleaded with us many times to turn back to Him fully, but we disregard the message. And now a time is coming when He will no longer protect us from our enemies.'

'What do you mean?' His words alarmed me.

Micah sighed heavily, as though he carried a heavy burden. 'I believe the enemy will take our people captive, remove them from their homes and take them to another land. Exile.'

As if my own escape to safety was hard enough. Would I now be taken further away from my family? Torn away from everything I knew? The thought sickened me. 'When will this happen?' I wanted to know exactly, so I could figure out a way to hide.

'Soon.' He gave a short laugh. 'But soon could be next month, next year, or a few score years away. I urge you to not spend time fretting over this, but rather serving the Lord with your whole heart. Who knows, but he might spare you further suffering?

'The main thing to remember is that Messiah *will* come. *He will stand and shepherd his flock in the strength of the LORD, in the majesty of the name of the LORD his God. And they will live securely, for then his greatness will reach to the ends of the earth.*'

I studied him as we climbed the mountain. Then, the truth dawned on me. 'That is the message you are going to speak in Jerusalem. About exile. About war. You are a prophet. Yes?'

Micah nodded slowly. 'Some have called me this, yes.'

I imagined that some people would be very unhappy to hear words of correction spoken to them. And words of warning. Would Micah be ignored? Cursed? Beaten?

'Are you not afraid?'

He shrugged again. 'Sometimes. But as I suggested for you, I focus on the Lord. *As for me, I watch in hope for the LORD, I wait for God my Saviour; my God will hear me.*'

***

The sun was setting as we neared Hebron's gates. Within a short time those gates would close to me. For the night. Perhaps forever, if my uncle waited there for me. I must have slowed my steps in hesitation despite the urgency, for Micah pressed his hand into my back urging me forward.

'It will be well, son. Make haste.'

The stone walls glowed yellow as the sun dipped towards the horizon behind us. Even so, they loomed above me, seeming impenetrable. The source of refuge that looked unreachable. Could I pass inside those walls to safety? I could make out the forms of several men standing about the gate. Dotan? My stomach turned in knots and my knees felt wobbly.

'I can't do this. I'll never make it.' I gasped, ducking into the shadows beside the road. My feet froze to the spot and my heart raced.

This was it. This would be my end. I would never see my family again. My friends. My cousins. All was lost. I would never take my father's place running the fields, trading the wheat. I would never marry or have my own children. All because of one selfish decision. *Abba in heaven, I am so sorry.*

'Yitzhak!' Micah's voice broke into my racing thoughts. He was waving his arm furiously at me. 'Come.'

I had not noticed a trader there, packing up his wares into a cart by the side of the road. I forced my uncompliant feet to stumble over to him.

'This is Elazar,' Micah introduced. 'He is heading into Hebron now. He will hide you beneath the covering of his cart.'

I looked at the man whose face was weathered by the sun, and I was sure, weathered by the storms of life too. He did not smile, he merely nodded to me. I turned to Micah and gripped his cloak. 'What if they inspect the cart?'

'I shall distract those at the gate.'

'But what if I accidentally give myself away, sneeze, cough or something?'

'I trust you will not.'

'Micah, I…' I could not put into words the terror I felt.

He looked me keenly in the eyes, stooping down a little to do so. 'Remember. You must trust in the Lord. He is your true refuge.'

I drew a deep breath and nodded. 'I will try.'

'Goodbye my young friend, Yitzhak,' Micah ruffled my hair. 'I shall pray for your health and prosperity.'

'Thank you, Micah. For everything.'

Elazar lifted the hide covering and I scrambled beneath it, curling into a ball, as small as I could. Micah instructed him to wait a few minutes so that he could go on ahead, and then there was silence. Except for the whistling. Elazar began to whistle as he led his donkey toward the gates of Hebron.

I heard a noise which became clearer as we neared the city entrance. It was not long before I realised it was Micah, his voice booming. I held my breath as we passed by the ruckus, afraid to move in the slightest, lest I be discovered. At first, I was certain Dotan was arguing with him, demanding he hand me over, but as I listened, I realised this was not the case.

'Woe to those who plan iniquity, to those who plot evil on their beds! At morning's light they carry it out because it is in their power to do it. They covet fields and seize them, and houses, and take them. They defraud people of their homes, they rob them of their inheritance.

Therefore, the LORD says: 'I am planning disaster against this people, from which you cannot save yourselves.''

I grinned to myself, despite my fears. That would get their attention. Micah was prophesying. Then it struck me. He risked his life, not just for my sake, but he would do the same wherever he went. Those words he spoke would make people angry. No. Furious. His fate was as perilous as mine. And yet he walked in faith and trust.

I was still pondering this when Elazar pulled back the cover and light met my eyes. I froze in fear. Why would he do that? Why would he expose me to my uncle? I must have flailed my arms around in panic, trying to pull the hide back over me, for Elazar laid a steadying hand on my shoulder.

'It's all right, son. We're inside the city.'

'What? We are?' Surprise and relief hit me at once and I began to cry again. I jumped from the cart and sank to my knees on the dusty street and thanked God for bringing me to safety. I remembered Micah's words – *the Lord is your true refuge* – and I felt them settle in my bones. My journey was far from over, but for now I was safe. Whatever may come, I would put my trust in the Lord, for *the name of the LORD is a strong tower; the righteous run to it and are safe.*

My Brother's Keeper

Valerie Volk

'But I want you to know that the Son of Man has authority on earth to forgive sins.' So he said to the man, 'I tell you, get up, take your mat and go home.' He got up, took his mat and walked out in full view of them all. This amazed everyone and they praised God, saying, 'We have never seen anything like this!' – Mark 2: 10-12

If I did not feel so damnably guilty, I would not be doing this. I would not be here on a hot summer afternoon, with half the population of Capernaum, I swear, all gathered around to stare and listen.

But he'd begged me, and I could not refuse.

That's the trouble. When you've harmed someone, when you're responsible for ruining their lives, you're never free. You have to repay. Again and again. It never goes away. You're never able to let go.

It was my doing; I always knew that. He doesn't need to say anything. Every time I catch a glimpse of that broken body, the same tide of guilt swamps me. There is no way I could deny him anything he asked.

Trouble was he'd always wanted to be like me. Now there's an irony. Because he wanted to be like me, he ended up the way he is. A shell of a man.

When they carried him back to the house, no one thought he would live. For many years he said it would have been better if he'd been killed outright. Not left like this. Sometimes I thought the same, when the black mood was on me. When I thought how different my life too would have been if he had died.

But he was my brother. He IS my brother, and I love him.

Does he too wake in the night, with the scene etched in his mind? The group of us, stupid youngsters that we were, daredevils, so proud of the things we got up to. Daring ourselves on to one mad act after another that summer. Convinced we were indestructible, that we could do anything we wanted.

Four of us, always together. Matthew, Simeon, Ezra and I. All the same age, at that time of life when you have everything ahead of you. We'd escape the synagogue and the classroom at the end of lessons, and the old Rabbi would watch us go, rolling up the Torah scrolls, shaking his head, wondering what devilment we were up to.

We'd grown tired of the games of our childhood. We were no longer interested in hide and seek, or the knuckle-bones and bull-roarers that used to sing in our hands. These days we'd mark out a sand grid for board games, or spend hours inventing new and more elaborate rules for the ball games we loved. But exploring – that was our chief delight. Plenty of opportunity in the hilly country around us, with caves to investigate.

As soon as we could dodge the demands of parents, for our fisherman fathers would ask help in net-mending, and our mothers at the threshing floor or the olive mills, we'd escape to the freedom of the countryside, and the adventures we could find.

Daredevils? Yes, we were. Driving each other on with more and more demanding challenges. We were a group, the four of us, and other village boys saw us as leaders. They tried to tag along, but we shook them off. Well, most of them. Except Eli, my little brother.

'Get him to leave us alone,' the others would urge. I tried my damnedest to send him home, but he'd trail along after us. Two years younger, and what a difference it made. Incessant, his asking.

'Can I come? Can I join your gang?'

'Where are you going?'

'Can I do it too?'

Or my mother's urging: 'Take your brother with you, Joseph!'

We fobbed him off with some of our old toys; for a time, my old, wheeled cart kept him happy, or Simeon's spinning top and hoop, but then he was there again.

'Let me come. Let me join your gang.' Over and over.

He trailed us out to the hills and watched us on the cliffs daring each other to new feats of jumping. His whining was endless. I should have ignored him, been stronger; I wasn't. I told him he could join us if he proved himself worthy.

The eagerness on his face still haunts my nightmares. 'What must I do?'

We looked at each other. 'A big jump.'

He was so ready. 'Where?'

I still don't know what made me point to the last cliff point, but I swear I never thought he would do it. It was a leap none of us would have tried. Sheer cliff – and a long, long drop.

We went on constructing the hut we were making in the undergrowth and forgot him. Until he called.

'Watch me do it.'

We froze in horror, then ran to stop him. But too late. The small figure had vanished. We reached the edge of the cliff and saw his small body, way below.

You can see why I will never stop feeling guilty.

When the men brought back the small broken body the Rabbi, at first, thought he would die. And that it might be best if he did. We had no physician, but our Rabbi was skilful in healing, and claimed power only from Jehovah in the cures he achieved. But this was beyond him. The small body was mangled beyond repair and the two legs totally useless. A type of palsy; from his hips down he was completely paralysed.

For days he hovered between life and death, and I did not know which I should beg for. Which would be worse? I was racked with guilt. My words. My pointing. My fault.

When his eyes finally opened, he looked at me and smiled. 'I did it, Joseph. I jumped.'

I knew then that I could never leave him. All these years I have cared for him, for when first my father, then my mother, died, they left him in my protection. I could not have refused. Because of me he was a half man, dependent on others for everything.

His life finished that day on the cliff top. Paralysed, legs completely useless, he could work a little with his hands. Between us we kept my father's small wood carving shop open. But he could in no way manage without me. His daily needs were my responsibility.

My life also finished that day on the cliff top.

My friends began to court village girls, and then to marry. I looked at Hannah, who blushed and smiled when she came into my shop, and made it clear that she looked on me with fondness. In the nights I dreamed of her and imagined she was in my bed…

Then rose from my couch to go to Eli, who needed me several times each night. My days were focussed on him. What right did I have to ask anyone to share this life? I sighed as Hannah's sister set up life with Malachi in one of the small houses between the synagogue and the lake. Hannah lived with them; she didn't marry.

Malachi shook his head when he looked at me. It was crowded with an extra woman in their small home. It was part of the block of houses around a courtyard, next door to another owned by big Simon, the man they called Simon the Fisherman.

Except that he'd stopped fishing. He was one of that group who had downed tools and gone off with the wandering preacher, the carpenter from Nazareth, who was drawing huge crowds with his speeches. With his actions too, for the stories they told of things he did had everyone talking.

I took little notice, because we were occupied with much work. But Malachi came frequently to our shop. As did the other two; Simeon and Ezra. The four of us learned to look at each other and even at Eli without flinching. I think they shared my feeling. It was our doing, we knew. But mainly mine. I was the one who had pointed to the cliff top.

They brought us news of what was happening in the village, and how the whole area was full of stories about this carpenter. He upset people wherever he went with the things he said. Even in Nazareth, his home town, where he'd lived for almost thirty years. You'd think they would have given a local boy an easier run.

'But no,' said Ezra, 'they threw him out of the synagogue when he took his turn at reading from the scrolls.'

Eli was fascinated. 'Why? What had he done?'

'Well, instead of just reading – and that's all he was meant to do – he started to talk about what he'd read.'

'Like the Rabbi?'

'Worse. He read from the prophet Isaiah, and tried to tell them that the prophecies were about him.'

'Bet that didn't go down too well.'

'Almost a riot. They asked him who he thought he was. Him. The local carpenter!'

'They threw him out of the synagogue,' said Simeon. 'Some of them wanted to march him to the cliff and throw him over.'

He clapped his hand to his mouth. The cliff - we all knew what he was thinking.

Eli was unconcerned. 'Tell me more about this carpenter.'

'Amazing stories about him,' said Ezra. 'They say he's made blind people see, and deaf people hear. All sorts of stuff.'

'All sorts of impossible stuff!' Simeon threw his shoulders back and stared at us defiantly. 'You'd have to be Jehovah himself to do half of what they claim he does.'

'I'm starting to wonder,' Malachi scratched his head. 'You know where I live. Near big Simon?'

The others nodded.

'His mother-in-law was sick. My wife told me the story. Really sick. Bad fever. He brought the carpenter home to stay with them and – wait for it – he took her by the hand and she was better. Right away. Just like that.'

Eli was fascinated, leaning forward. 'Perhaps the other stories are true too.'

They left soon after, shaking their heads.

But the stories kept coming, and the gossip grew – and Eli got more and more involved. Too many stories. Crowds coming from all the surrounding villages. People cured of all sorts of problems. Madmen with devils, people with the dreaded skin disease, blind and lame …

It was then that I saw Eli's eyes begin to shine.

'Maybe me? Perhaps he could do something for me?'

I didn't want him getting false hope. 'Look at your legs.' I said it as gently as I could. We both looked down. Not just paralysed and useless but twisted and wasted. It would take more than a miracle worker to fix those.

The idea had caught him, though, and he couldn't let it go. I remembered the persistent little boy, always at me. Here he was again.

'You could take me to him.'

'Impossible. How could I get you there? And with the crowds he draws, you wouldn't get near him.'

But he kept on and on.

One day when the four of us were gathered, he went over it all again.

'He's healing others. You all said so.'

I cursed the day we'd ever told him about the carpenter.

'No way we could get you to him,' I insisted.

The other three looked at each other, then uneasily at me.

'Maybe we ought to try. We sort of owe it to him.'

That got me. Perhaps we did.

So that's what brought us here on this hot Capernaum afternoon. Eli stretched out on a mat, and the four of us carrying the corners. When we neared the house, we saw that we'd been right. The crowd was thick all around the doorway and out into the courtyard. Somewhere in one of the inner rooms, people packed shoulder to shoulder, was the carpenter.

'No chance,' I said, and watched Eli's face fall.

'Hold on,' said Malachi. 'There are stairs at the back of these houses. They go up to the roof.'

'So?'

'I reckon if we can get this thing up top, we might be able to do something.'

Mad idiot, Malachi. But Ezra and Simeon straightened their shoulders, and they were burly men.

Next thing we were manoeuvring that unwieldy mat up the back stairway – lucky it was as broad as it was – and onto the flat roof. Looked as if the family used it in the hot evenings. There were rugs and a low table. But no other way down.

'What now, you with all the answers?'

'Take a look at this roof. There are beams for the ceiling, but they're not too close together, and in between it's just thatch mixed with mud.'

Simeon looked excited. 'I reckon I can break this up without too much trouble.'

'Enough to let the mat down?' Ezra was uneasy. 'It's risky. Even if we rope it.'

'I don't care.' Eli was frantic. 'Do it. Let me down.'

So that's how we came to be carefully taking chunks out of a roof. Fortunately down below they were so absorbed in his talk that no one noticed. That is, until the mat came to rest right in front of the Teacher.

'Can you help him?' I called down.

Everything went silent. The people gaped like stunned fish at the sight.

The Teacher looked up at me, and then at Eli.

'My son, your sins are forgiven.'

I swear he was speaking to me as much as to my brother.

There was a faint rumble in the crowd, where some of the learned men were sitting. 'Blasphemy,' I heard one say. And another, 'Only God can forgive sins.'

Didn't rattle the Teacher at all. He looked at them calmly. 'Is it easier to say to this man, 'Your sins are forgiven' or to say 'Get up. Pick up your mat, and walk'?'

Eli's eyes were shining, fixed on the Teacher with heart-breaking hope.

The crowd watched uncertainly.

'I will show you that I have the power to forgive sins.' The Teacher raised his eyes to the roof, past me, to the heavens – then spoke once more to Eli. 'I tell you, get up, pick up your mat, and go home.'

The people parted like the Red Sea, but not a word was spoken as my brother walked between them, his legs strong, carrying the mat, through the room, out the door, across the courtyard, on his way home.

I still wonder. Was it to Eli alone, or also to me, that the Teacher said 'Your sins are forgiven'?

My heart is lighter than it has been for many years.

L'Mort de Lazaraus

V. M. Cherian

Jesus said to her, 'I am the resurrection and the life. The one who believes in me will live, even though they die; and whoever lives by believing in me will never die. Do you believe this?' – John 11:25-26

The doorway into Sheol opens only once in front of a man, and there is no compromise when it does. You must pass through it whether you like it or not. It opens on its own accord at unexpected times; no man can command it. There are no exits. Once you are in, you are nothing more than a memory to the living; a silent sprite who endures in the shadow, forever separated from the light.

I saw the door a week before my death. It appeared so suddenly in my room as I lay in bed, terribly sick and burning with fever. Its appearance was faint at first, hardly more than a dream existing in another realm. But as I watched, it started growing before my eyes, ever looming closer and becoming more corporeal in form. It looked ancient and black, as though it was fashioned out of darkness itself. Strange runes were carved upon it, and before it, the angel of death stood, silently watching me. Waiting.

My fate was sealed. I just didn't know when. For now, the door was still closed. On the day it opened wide, that was when I would go. Every second passed by in constant terror. My sisters, Mary and Martha, who knew nothing of my visions, still held on to hope. They sat on either side, tending to me day and night. I didn't have the heart to tell them it was all futile.

My greatest regret is that I would have to leave them alone in a patriarchal society that largely excluded women. Who would protect them once I was gone? It was the curse of the women of my time: to be shut up in social prisons made by the rabbis. I knew Martha would be fine. She learned duty on our mother's lap. She did not aspire. She knew her place, and so she dutifully did what was expected. She stayed in the background, always serving, caring, nurturing, never speaking out of turn, and never seeking a place above men. She only sought to please. No, she would never be shunned.

But my Mary... Ah, I was worried about her. She was the opposite of Martha and hence a constant annoyance to her. As ardently as Martha clung to the societal norms, Mary silently defied them. She loved learning and knowledge more than domestic chores. Her sharp mind never rested from gleaning information, and her foresight was great. She longed to sit with men as their equals and learn the Tanakh from the rabbis. However, no one allowed her to go further than the women's courts at the Temple. Her strangeness made her a social pariah. She bore it all in her quiet taciturn way. But I knew she was miserable inside, trapped without any means of escape. I tried to alleviate her pain as much as possible. I let her be herself when she was away from the prying eyes of society, and she was always grateful for that little kindness.

I knew they would both be inconsolable once I was gone. Still, it would be Mary, not Martha, who would fade away and be lost if I was not there to anchor her. For Martha, I was just a beloved brother whose passing would be grievous. For Mary, I was more than a dear brother. I was also the source of her freedom—someone who saw and understood her without judgement.

I mustered all my strength to form words. I was too weak, and every effort was a terrible strain for me. Still, I had to prepare Mary for my death, maybe strengthen her and encourage her to find a way to move on.

'Mary...' My voice was raspy. 'I don't have many days left.'

She hushed me before I could speak my mind. 'You need to keep your strength. You are going to get well … You must ...' Her voice broke. 'I have sent word to Yeshua about your illness. I am certain that he will heal you.'

'Yeshua …will…come?'

'I am sure of it. He loves you.'

Hope surged in me. Yeshua was a great rabbi known all over Judea as a miracle-working prophet. He was also my closest friend. He had great power. I had heard tales of him even raising the dead to life. Rumours were going around that he was indeed the Messiah sent from God. I was confident that he could save me if he wanted to. Would he come in time?

Days passed. My condition was steadily deteriorating. I no longer felt connected to my body. For hours, I wandered to strange places in a feverish haze. The door was always before my eyes now. It was no longer closed. A wide crack had appeared along its periphery. The angel of death still stood before it. His dark sword was now unsheathed. It glinted red in the firelight. Strange runes were written on the blade too. It looked like the same ones as on the door.

I did not have any more time. Yeshua had yet to come to see me. Now I was sure he would not come. The messenger that Mary had sent to Yeshua had returned late last night. Martha had been the one who received him. As she served him dinner, he told my sisters that he had met with the Lord. Yeshua would come, he had said. However, he would not come right away. He planned to stay where he was for two more days before coming here.

'Two more days? Didn't you tell him how serious my brother was?' Mary had asked. They had been talking in whispers in the other room. But I could hear every word like as though I was there. Was I there? I couldn't be sure anymore.

'I did,' I heard the messenger say between bites. 'He knows Lazarus is about to die. Still, he has decided to set out only after two days. Perhaps he means for your brother to die. That might be God's will.'

Mary had been distraught when she heard that. I listened to her loud wails in the other room. Martha had tried her best to calm her down. But she would not be comforted. I watched her now as she sat beside me, still as stone, eyes staring vacantly into space, lips moving wordlessly in prayer. She looked utterly defeated as though even her last hope was taken from her. Occasionally, her trembling hands reached out to put a damp cloth on my hot, burning forehead. Martha was also grieving in her way. Even though she tried her best to hide her tears, she was not as strong in hiding her emotions as Mary was. Often, she would rush into the kitchen when the grief was too much for her, on the pretext of checking on the servants. I knew she was going in there to cry.

I didn't know what hope I could give both of them. I had lost the last ray of hope I had. Even if Yeshua arrived, I would be dead for more than two days. I did not think even he, God's messenger could bring a decomposing body to life. Only God could do that. The fact that he delayed his visit indicated that he knew God intended for me to die. That was that. I shall go to rest with my fathers, hopeless and in despair. My sisters would be orphans now; I had no words of comfort for them. They must fare as best as they can. Whatever cup God poured out for them, be it good or bad, they were bound to drink it. *Oh, God! May their fates be merry and without many shadows!*

The crack in the door was now widening. The door now stood fully open. The entrance was covered in a veil of light. I could not see what was on the other side. The angel of death came toward me, beckoning. *It is time!* It was the first time he spoke. His voice was almost like a hiss. I felt a strange urgency in my spirit to leave when he said the words. A call was sent out, and I had to answer. The runes on the door and the angel's blade glowed brightly for a second as though a decree was activated. As I watched, the angel thrust his sword into my body. I felt my spirit break away. My body lay on the bed like discarded rags. For a minute, I could hear the faint cries of my sisters. Then all was suddenly dark. I breathed no more.

***

Sheol, from where I stood, was a place of forgetfulness and rest. It existed in the middle of nowhere. It had no substance or form. Only shadows. The moment I passed through the door, I noticed the immense silence and sleepiness that it seemed to exude. I was not alone. Two men in shining white robes were blocking my way.

'Lazarus.' one of them said. 'It is time to rest. We have come to take you into Paradise.'

I followed them. They took me into a garden of sorts. It was one of the many tiers of Sheol. There were seven such tiers, each separated by the vast chasm that no one could cross. I was standing on the third tier. Below me was a fiery pit of torment. Gehenna. The place of the wicked. Far below this stood the bottomless abyss, where all the cursed angels were chained. Everything I was taught about the place of torment did not prepare me for the horror I saw. The fires of Gehenna were always burning. I could hear the anguished screams of the souls lost in there. I saw burning men and women pleading with God for mercy. They begged him for another chance- anything at all to get them out of there. Their pain welled up inside me. I cried at the sight. One of the angels who walked beside me touched my eye. Suddenly a fog surrounded us such that I could neither hear nor see the horrors anymore.

The angels were taking me deeper into the heart of the garden. I looked around me as I walked. It was a beautiful place. The grass was lush and green. Flowers of every kind grew there. It was peaceful and quiet. Yet there was darkness here as well. Paradise was not a place of torment, but it was also not a place of happiness.

As we reached the heart of the garden, I saw a beautiful tree standing there. Its leaves were lush, and they shone like radiant emeralds. On its branches were seven different kinds of fruits. Two angels, who looked like they were the guardians of the tree, stood before it with flaming swords. I was about to walk toward the tree to get a closer look when one of the angels stopped me.

'Stop! The path to the tree of life is denied to mortal men. The cherubim will destroy anyone who dares to go near it. Come. We must press on.'

Dejected, I followed the angels and we continued walking once more. The angels led me to a quiet corner. A cage stood there. It was fashioned with every evil I had committed while I was on Earth. Here I was to lie for all eternity till the judgement. I was alone. The angels left me there and flew heavenwards. Four more tiers stood above the garden where I sat. I did not know what three of the four tiers contained. I could not see them. A thin, impenetrable veil surrounded the final tier. Above it sat the glorious throne of God. Great light and joy were coming from the throne room. But I could not look there directly because the veil covered it. God's brightness and glory did not come down to where I was. This was the darkness that all men endured in paradise. To be separated for all eternity from the light of God.

I was in despair. Besides me, many cages sat like mine. In all of it, there were men and women. All of them were in a deep sleep. It was not a comfortable sleep. They all despaired at the darkness that seemed to surround them. Yet none could escape from it.

I do not know how long I sat there. Already a great weariness was coming upon me. I forgot things from my earthly life. Just for a moment, I thought of my sisters. As darkness covered my eyes, even they faded from memory. Soon I would be one of the shadows—not speaking, thinking, or living.

Suddenly a bright light shone before me. It was coming closer and closer. My drowsy eyes were opened at the sight, and I suddenly remembered who I was. I saw that the light coming toward me was a human man with radiant garments. As he approached me, I saw the veil surrounding the throne vanish for a second. The seraphim and the cherubim now stood silent, watching intently at what was happening in the garden. The man now stood directly before me. He looked familiar. It was Yeshua. I was stunned. How did he come here? What power does he possess that all of heaven would watch him in awe?

For a while, he said nothing. He just wept. He was in pain. He was crying for me. It was then that I saw his love for me in full. At his tears, all of heaven was in dismay. Then suddenly, he got up. He was saying something I could not hear. At his words, the heavens shook. Then I saw him raise his hands. From his mouth, I heard a loud command: 'Lazarus! Come Forth!'

All of Sheol trembled. The angel of death cowered in fear. I saw the doorway open again. This time, it was opening outwards. Now, I could see everything happening on Earth. My body as it lay decomposing in the tomb, Mary and Martha as they stood in their mourning clothes, wonderstruck at what was happening in the tomb. It was like our eyes were looking at the same thing from two sides of the doorway. A big crowd had gathered, and in the centre stood Yeshua, glorious in his appearance. I slowly walked toward him. My eyes went dark for a moment as my feet crossed the door threshold.

When the darkness lifted, I was back in my body again. My face was covered with a white cloth, and my hands and legs were tied. Still, with all my energy, I walked toward Yeshua. At his command, someone removed my bonds. When I could see again, I was standing in the sunlight outside the tomb. The darkness of Sheol had vanished. I was elated to be back in the land of the living. Mary and Martha ran toward me and hugged me. It was so good to see them again. Everyone who was mourning was now laughing and dancing. My heart was whole with joy and thankfulness.

***

It took me a while to fully understand everything that happened after I was gone: my death, burial, the arrival of the Lord, and the sorrow of my sisters. When I did, I praised God for all the kindness he showed me. I wanted to talk to Yeshua about everything. I went to him late at night as he sat alone. The disciples had all fallen asleep. He was waiting for me. He looked so human, so vulnerable. Nothing like the glorious being before whom the angels trembled, and death fled. I was still in shock and horror at what I saw in Sheol.

'Lazarus, you are full of questions!' He knew my mind.

'I saw all the righteous sitting in darkness, reserved for judgement.'

'Yes, the punishment for sin is great.'

'Is there then no hope for humanity? Are we all eventually going to be cast into the abyss with the angels of darkness?'

'Do not be afraid, Lazarus. I am the resurrection and life. Anyone who believes in me, even if he dies, he will live.'

'What does that mean, Lord?'

'Go in peace, Lazarus. Forget what you have seen. Very soon, I will go into Sheol myself, and then the very foundations of death will be destroyed. No longer will the dead die without hope.'

'Lord, please do not send me back to the hopeless place of mourning.'

'Do not be troubled. The next time you die, you will not be walking in the darkness alone. You will be with me in Paradise. Not the Paradise you have seen. But a Paradise where the tree of life is no longer guarded. You will walk in the very presence of God and his holy angels.'

It was a promise. Suddenly I longed for the day when all he said would come to pass.

As if he read my mind, he said, 'Soon.'

For a brief second, I saw him as I did in Sheol. God who came in the flesh; glorious, radiant, and eternal.

Faith Like a Child

R. A. Stephens

Then people brought little children to Jesus for him to place his hands on them and pray for them. But the disciples rebuked them. Jesus said, 'Let the little children come to me, and do not hinder them, for the kingdom of heaven belongs to such as these.' – Matthew 19: 13-14

Josiah's favourite chore was to feed the smallest calf, the one that needed special attention and extra care. He would stand on one of his father's stools and look directly in their eyes. He would gently rub their cheeks and watch each calf still its trembling. Each calf trusted Josiah's touch and with his gentle care they grew. Rebekah, his older sister, said he was a calf whisperer. It made him feel useful – and tall.

But he was not tall, he was small. Small and sick.

Josiah tried to help, tried to be useful. 'I can do it,' he would say over and over again. But when he helped to feed the bigger cows, they knocked him into the mud, every time.

Being small was hard. He did not grow as fast as other children his age. He was nine years of age and yet he wasn't much taller than five-year-old Joshua from the neighbouring farm.

He wanted to help Rebekah but mostly she helped him. She helped him when he dropped the cows' food, she picked him up when he fell in the mud, she wiped his brow and fed him soup when he was sick.

Rebekah did everything that their mother had done – until she and their newly born brother had died. Josiah tried not to remember his father's crumpled face as he covered up his mother's body with the baby next to her. It brought only sadness and tears – and pain.

Rebekah would recite stories of his parents to Josiah who was too young to remember.

'They would check the fields together, often hand in hand.' Rebekah would hold Josiah's hand and comfort him each time he was sick.

Soon Rebekah would have to make a family of her own. She would have to marry. She would not be with them forever. Josiah had to be useful. He had to help his father and Rebekah.

'I can do it,' he would say as he cleaned the house and swept the floor.

'I can do it,' he would tell his father as he lifted a large jar of oil for cooking.

'I can do it, I really can,' he would say as he balanced on another stool his father had made and reached for the cooking pot to make the evening meal. Enthusiasm shone through him for every task, except when he was just too tired. And when he was tired, he was sick.

But when he wasn't sick, Josiah travelled with his father to the market. They would take cows from the herd to sell and buy oil and grain and materials for the fields.

People crowded and shouted and argued. The noise beat at Josiah's head. The shouting shattered his ears. The smells turned his stomach. He tried to cut out the noise but could hear everything. He tried to stay enthusiastic, but it was always a challenge.

One day Josiah caught the conversation of the crowd.

'Have you heard about the people he has healed?'

'The blind, the lame.'

Josiah moved closer to hear more, while his father was buying grain nearby.

'He is coming to our town. He will be here in the coming days.'

'I want to hear him speak.'

'I just want to get close to him.'

'Who is he?'

People asked questions. Others answered, but their claims were hard to believe.

'He has come to save us all.'

'He will defeat everyone and take back what is ours.'

***

'Can we go see the rabbi when he comes, Father?' Josiah asked over the meal that night.

'He won't have time for children,' Rebekah said.

'What makes you say that?' Father spoke up.

'So many people want to see him. Adults always get first preference.'

Rebekah was right, but still Josiah was determined to see him. 'I can do it,' he said in his determined confidence.

***

All through the hard winter the stories of the prophet spread. Stories of miracles and healings. Finally, the news came: the prophet, Jesus, was coming to Josiah's town. Josiah woke at dawn to help his father feed the animals. He tended every calf and even fed the big cows. He only slipped once in the mud. And then they set off to the market.

'You are too little to see Jesus.' Rebekah looked around at the crowds. 'There are so many people. You will get sick again.' Josiah had only been well again a few days.

'I don't think the rabbi minds how big or little you are'. Josiah jumped up and down trying to see the prophet. 'He might even help me to grow taller.' Josiah seemed to stop and think. 'Perhaps he will stop me being sick.'

'I don't know ...' Rebekah said.

'Let's go together.' Josiah took his sister's hand, as she so often did for him, and weaved through the crowds/people.

There were men all around the rabbi. At least a dozen of them. They stood in the way, filtering who could see him.

'Slow down. one person at a time.'

'Children can wait.'

Josiah and Rebekah were not the only children. Many parents

were bringing their children. Some were sick, some were just curious. Most were dirty, covered in dust from having walked so far.

'This is no place for children,' One of the men waved them away.

Rebekah stopped. 'It's no use, Josiah. A little boy and a girl like me, not yet betrothed. They don't want us.'

'I can do it. I will see him,' Josiah whispered and pulled Rebekah forward. Again he pulled her hand.

'Let them come.' The voice was as powerful as a lion yet warm like a summer breeze. 'Let the little children come. Do not hinder them.'

***

He laid his hands on many of them and laughed. Parents were celebrating, children who were previously slumped had energy unlike before. The men standing around Jesus relaxed as well. Many people shake their hands.

'What if he touches me, Rebekah?'

Josiah's little hand grasped Rebekah's and pulled her along with all the enthusiasm his tiny body could muster. The line shortened and they could see Jesus clearly. He was sitting on the ground with children all around him. As soon as children left, others filled their place.

'Josiah, wait,' Rebekah froze.

'Don't be afraid.' Josiah looked at her, his vision blurred with tears of joy. 'He will make me better. I am sure.'

'With faith like that, for such a small boy, you will go far.' Jesus held out his hand and drew Josiah and Rebekah to sit beside him.

'Please Rabbi, can you help my sister?' Josiah's voice was not weak, his words did not waver. He could do this; he could speak to this revered rabbi. 'She is scared. She needs strength.'

'Do not fear, my child. Trust and have faith.' Jesus put his hand on Rebekah's head and tears flowed down her face like a river released.

'And for you ...' Jesus reached down and held Josiah's hand.

And Josiah grew. He grew tall and strong and took over from his father managing the pastures and herds of cattle. He never again fell in the mud, and he never stopped talking about the great rabbi, Jesus, who would talk to a small child, and who helped him grow.

Claudia Procula

Laura Motherway

While Pilate was sitting on the judge's seat, his wife sent him this message: 'Don't have anything to do with that innocent man, for I have suffered a great deal today in a dream because of him.' – Matthew 27:19

We arrived at Caesarea Maritima late in the afternoon. The heat was stifling but the breeze from across the ocean brought with it a familiar saltiness, for which I was grateful. I marvelled at the beauty of the vast coastline. It stretched as far as the eye could see. The city was itself a sight to behold. Sprawling and symmetrical with Roman engineering and palm trees where you might least expect to see them. The city started at the shore and felt sturdy and proud, as if it was challenging an opponent to a battle it couldn't lose. Or perhaps it was me who would engage in battle with this beautiful and mysterious place. At least, that is what is what my dreams had told me.

From as early as I can remember, I struggled to know my dreams from reality. They followed me throughout my waking hours, hovering over me like a thick mist distorting the thin line between reality and fantasy. I kept my dreams to myself. It felt safer. Sometimes they helped me decide something trivial or provided an insight into the trustworthiness of strangers, but for the most part, they seemed of little importance in my day-to-day life. As I grew older, I became more troubled by my dreams. Sometimes, I didn't dare sleep.

One dream haunted my childhood and continues even now. A newborn lamb, just learning to walk, fleece of the purest white, cleaner than any linen in the finest palace, comes towards me. Its large brown eyes gaze deeply into mine. I love this creature. It nestles into my hip. I drop to my knees and take its head in my hands and caress its soft wool. I close my eyes and feel the warm sun on my face and the breeze blowing against my body. When I open my eyes, my hands are overflowing with blood. The lamb lays slain at my feet. Its throat is cut and blood pours to the ground. I am alone in the field and stand in a pool of blood, until I can force myself awake.

As our ship docked, I looked at my husband. Our betrothal and marriage had been a whirlwind. I remember some moments vividly, but others I cannot tell if they were real or a dream. I remember the foreign touch of the fine silk of my tunic grazing my skin as it fell to the floor. It was too grand for someone like me. My childhood was spent in Ostia; I had more need for a fishing net than I did for beautiful clothes. In Rome, everything was different. Tiberius accepted me as his stepdaughter, and I was to be married to a legion legate recently returned from the Rhine. My future husband had impressed the emperor's advisors with his mind for military tactics and skills with the javelin and was to be rewarded with a marriage that would advance his career. For a short time, I stopped dreaming altogether.

The first time I saw Pilate, I found him striking. He was handsome, tall, and well spoken. He held himself with a confidence unlike most equestrian citizens. When he spoke, people listened intently. He held his gaze a moment longer than most. I could see why the senate was impressed; a man like that is an asset to Rome. I felt a panic of inferiority when I walked beside him the first time, but soon our conversation flowed easily. He attempted questions about my childhood and trivial interests, but I had always been more interested in deeper thoughts and shared, a little too freely, my ideas on politics and philosophy. Instantly, I regretted the audacity with which I had spoken but to my delight he seemed not to mind the way I spoke my truth. In fact, as I came to learn throughout the years to come, he admired it.

My husband was discerning and clever. I lapped up his intelligent words as though they came from Minerva herself, and he enthusiastically welcomed mine. Since boyhood, Pilate had studied and admired the military prowess of Julius Caesar, and I suppose my blood line was so impressive to him that he overlooked the deficiency of my gender and indulged me as an equal in political conversation in the privacy of our home.

Twelve years into Tiberius' reign, Pilate was summoned to Palatine Hill. Sejanus was doing most of the emperor's work in Rome and was impressed with the way Pilate brought order to the least organised legions during his time in the military. There had been much dinner party speculation about a new appointment. At first, I dismissed it as nothing more than gossip, but as it grew more frequent, I allowed myself to fantasise about a powerful posting somewhere exotic and beautiful. I enjoyed Rome, but I missed being close to the sea - the smell of the salty air, the sea birds, and the simple lives of the coastal village people. In the deepest chambers of my heart, I hoped it would be Greece.

'Judea,' said Pilate when he returned. 'The Governor is being removed and I am to take his place. We sail in two weeks.' I tried to hide my disappointment, but my husband knew me well. 'We will live in Caesarea. You will like it,' he smiled, 'it's near the sea.'

For the next seven years I relished every opportunity to learn about this strange place, and the Jewish ways and customs. I accompanied my maids to the market whenever I could and marvelled at the way their religion was part of their daily life, not just at times of worship. It was strange to think they worshipped only one God. Such commitment, such devotion, such piety. It was impressive. I stopped wearing my bullae to ward off evil spirits. Somehow, I felt I did not need it in Judea. I wish I had paid more attention to my dreams.

The lamb visited my dreams more and more often, unsettling me for days afterwards. I would look behind me at times, certain I would see the white, glowing fleece following me through the dusty streets. I developed an obsession with cleanliness, washing my hands so vigorously and often that the servants worried for my health. Following the birth of my two sons, I had the bed sheets burned, so troubled was I by the sight of blood. I could not bear sacrifices so I stopped attending the temple and feasts for fear of fainting. I could feel the lamb following me wherever I went, and I wanted nothing more than to escape its blood.

Pilate tolerated the Jewish people but never warmed to their ways. His job was to keep the order, collect taxes and represent the emperor's interest in Jewish affairs. My clever husband was a natural diplomat and for the most part, Israel and Samaria enjoyed relative order. Stationed longer than any governor before him, Tiberius was impressed with Pilate's diplomacy and commitment to order. Public disorder was a rarity, and taxes flowed reliably to Rome. He met regularly with the high priests and politicians. 'Temple money builds fine Roman aqueducts,' he would say when I asked about their meetings. Something within me told me it would be unwise to press further.

On a visit to Jerusalem, we attended a feast. A priest in black clothing approached and I recoiled, too slightly for anyone to see, but a wave of nausea gripped me from within.

'Joseph, allow me to introduce my wife, Claudia Procula,' my husband said. The old man sneered at me through his clenched smile, his repulsion palpable. I knew what he was thinking: the way Pilate considered me an equal at his side was an insult as well as an obstacle to be overcome. That night, I dreamed of Joseph Caiaphas and his sneering face covered in snakes. I woke in a sweat and told my husband what I had dreamed.

The longer we spent in Israel, the more tense things became. A political movement was breaking through. You could feel it in the air like a heavy heat or a fog that lingered, silent but dangerous. Even the might of the Roman army could not hold back what was coming. Pilate prided himself on his ability to keep peace and order, but riots were becoming more frequent. There was an increased resistance to paying taxes and public crucifixions, which once served as a deterrent to potential agitators, now seemed only to incite more unruly behaviour in the streets. It took its toll on my husband and it pained me see him struggling under such an enormous weight. He was looking older, more tired and his temper raged over the slightest irritation. Soldiers were flogged for minor transgressions and the crucifixions increased, as did pressure from the temple. The high priests insisted on meeting at all hours of the day and night, and Pilate obliged, bringing with him increased security. We were assigned twice as many Roman soldiers to our residence in Caesarea and while accompanying us on visits to Jerusalem.

The Passover festival always intrigued and excited me. I enjoyed how my Jewish servants prepared special meals and sacrifices and I asked endless times to hear the story of their prophet, Moses. But this time felt different. More dangerous. As though the world was teetering on the edge of a cliff and about to be thrown into the turbulent sea.

'You can stay in Caesarea this year, if you prefer.' My husband rubbed the back of his neck. 'Jerusalem grows more dangerous by the day.'

But something told me I needed to be in the city with my husband. I hadn't slept well for the past few weeks and my dreams were becoming more and more unsettling. Each night I dreamed my husband was falling from high above me and no matter how desperately I yelled, nobody would help me. I held out my arms, but he slipped through and he plummeted to the ground.

I breathed a silent sigh of relief when we arrived at the palace compound. The giant fortress felt safe, and I was anxious to be inside. For all his faults, the Jewish king Herod certainly had impressive architects. The compound walls towered above the city creating an impenetrable fortress, equal to the best in Rome. I was weary from the journey. 'Esther,' I called for my servant, 'my husband and I will require our meal an hour earlier this evening.' Pilate would be anxious to meet temple officials to finalise plans for the Passover festival and I was eager to retire early and rest. 'Of course, Mistress.' Esther had worked in the palace compound since we'd arrived in Judea all those years ago. She was competent, loyal, and kept a good ear to the ground for me. Her insight was invaluable.

That night sleep was elusive. My body was heavy with fatigue, yet my mind raced with thoughts and my heart threatened to burst through my chest. I clenched my eyes tightly, breathed deeply, drank goats' milk; all the things that usually helped my insomnia. When my mind quietened enough to sleep, the dream came. More vivid than any before, and more foreboding. The lamb. Of course it was the lamb. Nightly, it haunted my sleep but this time it transformed into a man. An enormous crowd gathered, more people than grains of sand on the seashore. They were the ancestors of all who had gone before and the unborn descendants of all who would come after. The man walked calmly across the heads of the crowd as though he simply walked through a pasture. He glowed pure and white, innocent as a newborn baby, and with the gentleness of a hen gathering her chicks beneath her wings. And then he was gone, and I was awake, soaked with sweat, trembling and breathless.

'Mistress?' Esther was surprised to see me awake so early and stumbling through the palace kitchen. 'Are you unwell? Or cold? You are trembling and all colour has gone from you.

Please sit down. Your husband has been called away urgently, but I will care for you.'

The songbirds were singing, but the day had not yet dawned. Esther seemed concerned and hesitated a moment before she spoke. 'The prophet, I mean, that man, the one the people come to listen to, the one from Nazareth, has been arrested overnight and is being brought before your husband this morning for judgement.'

My heart plummeted deep within, and I could not breathe. The blood left my fingers and toes and a strange vibration pulsed through my body. The room swayed before my eyes. I felt all the colour drain from my face. 'Mistress!' Esther sat me down and frantically instructed water to be brought.

'He can't,' I cried, without knowing why, 'He must have nothing to do with that prophet. Fetch me a messenger at once. I must get a message to my husband.'

I ordered the messenger to be insistent to deliver the message to Pilate. I looked directly into his eyes and pleaded with a desperation so foreign to me, it caught me by surprise. 'You must not fail.'

In all my life I have never felt so powerless. I paced the palace hallways, lamenting the futility of my position and praying to the gods I had long ceased to worship that the man from Nazareth would be freed. The moments became minutes, then hours. I could neither eat nor drink. I felt I was falling, but I could not sit. The faintness persisted and my breathing was shallow, as though a millstone was crushing my chest. The roar from the crowds in the street fuelled my fear and their cries threatened to engulf me.

At noon, the clouds blocked out the sun and, in a moment, the whole city was thrust into darkness as black as midnight. For three hours I waited, trembling and afraid until a thunderous sound jolted me, and my ears rang with the ferocity of the roar. I watched helpless, as a bolt of lightning split the temple in two, right down the middle. My heart tore in terror and I dropped to my knees at my window above the city, and begged mercy from a God I would yet come to know.

Burdens

Anne Hamilton

A certain man from Cyrene, Simon, the father of Alexander and Rufus, was passing by on his way in from the country, and they forced him to carry the cross. –
Mark 15:21

When Father returned, our worst fears were realised. He hadn't been drinking. One look at his sombre face and his terrifyingly sober eyes and my guts turned to water.

We weren't expecting him for several days, and that was our undoing. Alexander and I were enjoying a rare moment of ease, one we would never have dared snatch while Father was at home.

Mother had taken the cookpot out to our tiny back courtyard, seeking the early evening breeze off the shore. In the dying light, Xander and I were inside, and I was showing him a knot a sailor down at the docks had taught me. We should have been lighting the oil lamps—but we'd been distracted by our efforts to perfect the knot. If done right, it had a tight, firm tie but, with the right tug, it came easily undone.

I should have realised our danger when the last rays of sunlight from the outer door disappeared in an instant. However, the skies had been so strange in the previous week that it just didn't register. There'd been an unexpected eclipse accompanied by an eerie silence that lasted half an afternoon. Not a gull squawked, not a dog barked. The priests up at Apollo's temple had been frantic. I'd been at one of the side doors, selling dried fish, and witnessed their nervous fluttering. The sun-god vanishing without warning and without a cloud in the sky was a perilous omen.

Of course, the sudden darkness and the solemn stillness caused a fearful commotion at Cyrene harbour. Even the waves lapping at the shore seemed muffled by the gloom. None of the sailors would step foot aboard a ship when such a menacing portent was unfurled across the heavens. The passengers were no less jittery. It took three days for them to get over their fright, and then it was only after some serious sacrificing by the captains to the Dioscuri, the celestial twins who protect mariners from shipwreck.

The captains had just managed to satisfy both passengers and crew with some pre-dawn ceremonies when the earthquake struck. There was no prospect of a boat leaving harbour after that. Some of the more superstitious passengers went further up the coast to Balagrae, hoping to find a more auspicious place to board a ship for Athens. I escorted a party of them all the way, earning a double denarius for my efforts. It joined my secret hoard under the paving in the courtyard.

All my adventures in the last fortnight would have been forbidden if Father had been home. Selling fish to the temple priests, escorting the pilgrims to Balagrae, visiting the harbour, befriending the sailors. He told us to keep ourselves separate. 'Holy', he called it, 'a people set apart.'

As the light from the doorway vanished, Xander got up to light the lamp. I was still fiddling with the knot when I saw his face change. And I knew.

Father was home.

There had been no slam of door against the wall to warn us. No bellow of 'Alexander, Rufus!' No way we could have guessed. There were no ships were leaving Cyrene, so how could we have imagined that one would come sailing in?

I turned as Father entered the house, so quiet in his massive tread that his presence felt threatening. No, *more* threatening. He was a huge man, intimidating wherever he went. I don't ever remember a time when I wasn't scared of him. Terrified, to be honest. My dreams—daydreams and nightmares—always revolved around leaving home and escaping his brutal presence. The reason I hadn't, quite apart from not having enough saved to make my way past Tarshish to the Tin Isles at the end of the world, was that I was frightened of what might happen to Mother and Xander if I left. I knew he'd take out his fury on them.

Xander was standing, wide-eyed and stupid, frozen. And Father was facing us, staring, as if we were strangers and he was seeing us for the first time. He said nothing. Just peered around, taking the room in, in a strange and curious way. It was chilling. Even more chilling than one of his rare drunken rages. Mostly, when he was drinking, he'd fall into a half-stupor—difficult but, between us, Xander and I had learned to manage him.

It was the cold violence of his anger, untempered by the moderating influence of wine, that we'd grown to fear and hate.

'Mother,' I called, determined to warn her, 'Father has come home.' I kicked Xander and he stumbled to light the lamp.

Still Father said nothing. Mother scurried in, a fluster of veil billowing around her, a pot of hot spiced vegetables in her hands. 'Welcome, husband.' Her eyes didn't meet his. She put the pot on the table and I knew at once it wasn't enough. Mother would not eat tonight, and my portion and Xander's would be much smaller than she'd intended.

'It has been a long voyage.' Father spoke at last. 'I am tired and, if I tell you now of what has befallen me, I may misspeak and injure the story. I will see you in the morning.'

He was a dark shadow that passed by us towards his bed. We ate in total silence, only relaxing when we heard soft snores coming from his pillow. Mother sighed and Xander reached out his hand to cover hers. 'Perhaps the rabbinic court did not grant him a certificate of divorce, after all,' he whispered.

I was stunned. Certificate of divorce? Was that the real reason Father had gone to Jerusalem? Not the Passover at all? How did Xander know what I did not?

I felt torn. A divorce would be freedom from pain and fear. But it would also mean homelessness and destitution for Mother.

I woke the next morning to a fear-drenched atmosphere. Father was raking the embers of the fire, coaxing them back to life. But that was my job. If they were completely cold, I was to take a covered pot, hurry to the fire-kindler and bring back enough hot coals to warm Father's breakfast.

As if discovering Father doing my job wasn't alarming enough, I realised that Mother wasn't out at the well, drawing water. Instead there was a huge pot just inside the doorway, far too big for her to shoulder. Father must have brought it in. He dipped a ladle into it, dashed some water into a dish and then added crushed barley from the grain store. 'Come, Rufus, stir this...' He noticed me blinking, trying to rub the sleep out of my eyes. '...your mother needs a rest.'

He'd beaten her senseless. That was my first thought. But even as it flitted through my mind, she stepped into the room, looking around like a startled deer in the pre-dawn light, uncertain and flighty. She saw the waterpot and the fire, the dish and the barley, and was clearly as baffled as I was. 'What are you doing, Simon?' she asked Father.

'Giving you a day off,' he said.

The world had flipped upside down. I had no pattern in which to process his words. I stared. Mother gaped.

And Xander clattered in, breaking up the awkward moment as he brought an armful of firewood from the courtyard. That was another of my jobs. My heart drummed in sudden fear. The paving stone hiding my secret hoard was right by the wood stack.

Not a word was spoken. Father simply put out his hand and gestured mother towards the outside stairway leading to the roof. I didn't see them again until after lunch and neither did Xander. And when I did, I could tell right away Mother had been crying. That worried me because the unspoken rule we always abided by was this: never show tears in front of Father. It only escalates his rage.

I spent the morning by the docks, gleaning news, helping patch a net, getting paid in half a dozen fish. One of the fishermen scaled them for me and I took home the fillets at lunchtime. It seemed the ship Father had arrived in was still in harbour, needing some sails fixed, and wouldn't be making the return voyage to Joppa until the following day.

Ah, Joppa. I was reminded of the story of Jonah that we read every year on Yom Kippur. Joppa was the port he'd left from, as he ran from God's calling to Tarshish at the edge of the world. I sighed to myself, rueing that the boat wasn't heading west to the Pillars of Hercules, let alone as far as Tarshish or the Tin Isles.

I took the fish home. Father was cooking and said, 'Thank you,' for the fillets. I was so astonished, I almost ran back to the safety of the harbour. But I wanted to find Xander. He was nowhere around and I didn't dare ask. Mother, red-eyed and sniffly, was stripping herb leaves for the stew Father was concocting. She smiled at me, tentative but unguarded. It was so unnerving.

The world, always a dark and scary place, had become oppressively so.

The stew was filling and delicious, but I found myself almost choking on it. I went back to the harbour, and found a fisherman who wanted to head out to the oyster rocks. I was willing to go, but made sure I wasn't going to be paid in oysters. They're not kosher. I wasn't willing to risk Mother's ire, let alone Father's, by coming home with shellfish. Of course, there was always the chance of a pearl. That was my dream. I could take Mother with me to Tarshish if The Name, blessed be He, favoured me with a snowgem of the sea.

We were coming into shore, my head aching from sunlight splintering on the water and from more than two dozen dives near the reef to harvest plump oysters and mussels, when I saw my parents walking along the beach. They didn't see me, but I watched them all the way in—earning more than a few curses from the fisherman who wanted more rowing than gawking.

Maybe they were working out the terms of the divorce. It happened occasionally, but very rarely. Everything depended on the rabbi who signed the paper. Some were much stricter than others.

I was late arriving home. I needed to change the denarius I'd received into four sestertii, so I could add to my hoard but give Father most of my earnings. It took a while before I found someone willing to do it without a fee. The parents were out, but Xander was home and well-fed. 'They said not to wait up,' he informed me, throwing a still-warm hunk of bread in my direction.

'What on earth is happening?' I asked.

'No idea.' He shrugged.

I wanted to strangle him but I was so tired after the day, my head still thumping, that I lay down early. I wasn't intending to sleep but, next thing I knew, it was morning. I scrambled out of bed, ready to check the embers and stoke the fire, but again it wasn't necessary. Mother was up this time, cooking breakfast far earlier than usual. The waterpot was full, the firewood gathered.

Her quizzical look at me was unsettling.

'What's going on?' I asked her.

She reached out and ruffled my hair. 'You're a good boy, Rufus. A kind child. Have I ever told you that I'm proud of you?'

The world did another tilt. 'Not in as many words,' I said.

145

'But I knew it.'

Her sudden smile was radiant. I'd never seen how beautiful she was before that moment.

'Where's Xander?' I asked.

'Talking with your father.'

I gulped down the barley pap she'd made and flung myself out of the house. The tension was too much for me. I don't remember that day. I have no idea whether I worked at the harbour or went up to the silphium fields and spent a day harvesting herbs or if I helped load a donkey train for the Greek traders coming through. There's no memory at all.

I was a ragged wreck of foreboding, waiting for the explosion. I couldn't rest easy, couldn't feel safe, couldn't feel peace, until the volcano blew its top and I could assess the damage. I was stuck in the calm before the final eruption.

As soon as I could get him alone, I asked Xander what Father had spoken to him about. 'Not for me to say.' His nonchalant shrug was maddening, infernally irritating. Then he smiled. 'I think he has changed, Rufus.'

The only time in my life I've ever came close to punching my brother was that moment. There'd been times before when we hoped Father had changed but they never lasted. Never.

I knew the next morning it would be my turn on the roof. I just knew it. I thought of taking my hoard and making a run for it, but it was pointless. I had a sleepless night as I considered my options. Where could I go that I wouldn't be recognised and brought back before the day was out? And if I actually got past places where I was recognisable, chances were my money would be stolen and I'd be taken as a slave.

I couldn't eat the next morning. I knew I'd throw up.

The sun was sickeningly bright when Father suggested we go up to the roof. There we sat, facing each other, on the summer sleeping couches. He searched my eyes. I searched the horizon for boats on the water, for escape, for hiding places.

At last Father spoke. 'Rufus, my son…' His voice was quiet, almost gentle. 'My beloved son, I…' His eyes must have held some mesmeric magnetism because my head jerked around and my gaze locked on his. 'I am sorry,' he said.

I started to shake. I felt my left leg quiver and I mentally ordered it to stop, but it rebelled against me.

'I am sorry,' Father repeated. 'I've wounded your soul. I wanted you to be strong and courageous, so I thought I had to be hard on you. This was wrong of me…'

There was nothing in my stomach, but I was heaving, heaving, heaving—ready to throw up. I was trembling so badly that the savage earthquake of the previous week was like a shiver on a frosty night by comparison. Panicking, frenzied, I jumped up, ready to run. But I was shaking too much to stay upright.

Father caught me in his arms. Held me. Held me, even when I struggled. Held me and wouldn't let go.

There was a strange sound coming from one of us. I thought at first it was me, sobbing, then I realised it was Father. 'Oh, Rufus, Rufus,' he wept, 'I knew I had hurt you but I never imagined it was this much.'

I was still shaking. And I was desperate to leave. Of all the unbearable experiences of my life, I never thought an apology would be the worst. But Father had me in his arms, caged, and he wasn't about to set me free.

His sobbing subsided at the same time as my trembling did, and he held me at arm's length, looking me in the eyes. 'Promise you won't run,' he said.

It was the last thing on earth I wanted to give my word on, but I nodded. Gulping, I sat back down. There was a vile taste in my mouth.

'My father always said a boy was like a bar of metal,' he went on. 'To temper it to the finest quality, you beat and turn, beat and turn, beat and turn.' He took a deep breath and there were tears glistening in his eyes. 'That was how he brought me up. I hated him…' He paused. '…so I know what you think of me.'

Did he expect me to deny it? I was trapped. The Torah said, 'Honour your father and your mother,' but it also said, 'Do not speak falsely.'

I took refuge in scowling silence.

And suddenly my father smiled. As if he'd read my mind and approved of my solution to the dilemma.

'Let me explain what has happened.' He paused. 'I went to Jerusalem to get some important documents attested. I was hurrying, because I wanted to complete what needed to be done before Passover and leave. However, as I was entering the city, I was pushed aside by a crowd coming out the gate. The Romans were crucifying a band of criminals. One of the condemned men fell just in front of me. And a centurion pointed to me, then to the crossbeam the man had dropped. He didn't say a word. I think I could have protested that it wasn't legal—I was only required to carry a soldier's pack for a mile, not a beam. But I could see the mood of the troops was ugly. They were calling for torches, but the pitch kept smoking without giving light. So they were frightened but naturally they couldn't admit it. The sky was slowly fading to black, yet no clouds covered the sun. It was like an eclipse, but unlike as well. The moon hadn't risen. The sun had simply veiled its eye. But no stars were appearing.'

I nodded, remembering the day. Over two weeks ago now. Up on the cliff, at Apollo's temple as I'd been delivering fish, I'd witnessed the priests cutting themselves in a fervour of bloodletting, trying to lure the sun-god back.

'I was intending to leave as soon as I got the crossbeam to its destination,' Father went on, 'but I stopped to read the sign showing what the criminal was charged with. It simply said, 'King of the Jews' in three different languages. I was so stunned, I looked at Him. And as the soldiers were nailing Him to the cross, He said to me, 'Thank you for carrying my burden.' The man's mother was there with several other women. I would have gone but I didn't like to leave them without a protector. Not with the darkness intensifying so deeply and the torches guttering so feebly. It was so hard to see it was some time before I realised the women actually weren't alone. Two members of the court of the Sanhedrin were there and one of the man's disciples. It was a hard dying, Rufus. I will spare you the details.'

I was glad of his reticence. Yet I wondered what Father was driving at with this story. What did this have to do with his change of heart?

'One of the Sanhedrin members asked me if I would stay until it was over, to help them take the body to a nearby tomb. I thought he could sign my papers for me, so I agreed. He said his name was Ben Gurion, but the others called him, 'Naqdimon."

Surprised into speech, I blurted out, 'You met Nicodemus?

You met the righteous miracle-worker, the Pharisee whose prayer God answered when the sun broke through?'

'I met more than Nicodemus, my son. I met the Messiah. Who is a much greater miracle-worker than Naqdimon has ever been. He's healed the sick, cast out demons, raised the dead, fed multitudes, walked on water.'

I blinked. Could it be true? Surely not. Wouldn't we have heard, even here in Cyrene?

'I do not think there are many men to whom the Messiah Himself has said, "Thank you." Tears were streaming down Father's face. 'I carried His burden for Him on the way to His death. I listened to His words as He died and I knew the reason why I had carried His burden.' He wiped his tears on his sleeve. 'So He could carry mine. And not just mine. But the sins of all the world.'

He reached out his hands and took mine. For the first time, I realised how scarred and calloused they were. 'He forgave me, Rufus. And when He'd died and one of the soldiers took a spear and plunged it into His side, blood and water poured out. I realised He'd died of a broken heart, and my heart broke too. In that moment, I forgave my father and I stopped hating him and I realised what I had done to my family.'

I didn't know what to do. I knew what I was supposed to say but the words choked in my throat. I couldn't forgive. Not now. Maybe not ever.

'There is more I want to say,' Father went on, 'but not to you alone.' His hands still holding mine, he pulled me to my feet and held me for a moment, before turning me towards the stairs. We went down to the courtyard where Xander and mother were waiting for us.

They were scanning my face. Hardening it to inscrutability, I stared back, trying to read their expressions. And then I realised. Xander had forgiven Father. All the years of brutality and ruthless cruelty—how could they suddenly be deemed as nothing? I felt so conflicted that I was angry with Xander. He made me ashamed of holding out and yet, at the same time, he made me proud of my stance. My heart was in turmoil.

Father cleared his throat. 'I want to go back to Jerusalem. I want to present you all to the Messiah, blessed be He.'

'I thought He was dead,' Xander said, sounding confused.

Exactly my thought. Hadn't Father just said He'd died of a broken heart?

'You are correct, Alexander,' Father said. 'He *was* dead.'

No, I thought. I am not going to fall into this trap. Let someone else take the bait.

Xander volunteered almost at once. 'You want us to meet a ghost?'

Xander's question was even more stupid than mine would have been.

'Of course not!' For a moment, we caught a glimpse of Father's old impetuous fierceness. Then it was gone. 'Did the earthquake reach this far?' he asked.

We all nodded.

'It was an angel, rolling the stone back from the tomb where we had laid the body of the Messiah, Jesus of Nazareth. That's what caused the earthquake.'

'Angel?' My mother sounded as dubious as I felt.

'I personally did not witness the event,' Father said, 'but I spoke to a woman who did see the angel. She also saw Jesus, alive and in the flesh, afterwards.' His voice was earnest and compelling but I was not convinced. He believed a woman? It was a testimony no rabbi would accept in a court of law. What had happened to my father, the inveterate stickler for legal niceties?

'You. Believe. A. Woman?' My mother said each word so slowly and distinctly I knew she was having difficulty processing the thought.

'Yes.' Father nodded, obviously eager to convince her. 'Jesus had many women among His disciples. Wealthy women, too. I met some during those long hours at the cross. I'm told He loves the company of children. I'm sure He would welcome Alexander and Rufus, and you too, Irene, as His followers.' His eyes had a strange pleading look in them. 'After all, He owes me a favour. And although I owe Him in return more than I can ever repay in this life, I'm sure He will not deny my request for a blessing for you all.' His voice dropped, gentled. 'Come to Jerusalem, my love. Come meet the Son of God Himself.'

I shook my head as tears welled in mother's eyes. 'Where will we get the money?' she whispered, her voice cracking. 'We are still in debt from this last trip.'

'The boys and I can work our way over.'

Actually, that could be fun.

'Rowing a galley?' Xander sounded horrified.

I wasn't thinking galley. More coast-hugging sailboat. A galley would be relentless hard work.

'You take the boys,' Mother said.

'I want you to come,' Father said.

'Not a galley,' Xander said.

'Maybe we should wait,' Mother said.

'There is urgency on my heart,' Father said.

'Not a galley,' Xander said.

'Next year, Jerusalem,' Mother said. 'It will give us time to save.'

'I feel we need to be there by Pentecost,' Father said.

'Not a galley,' Xander said.

'STOP!' I yelled. 'BE QUIET!' My soul was tearing in two. There are more ways of offering pardon than words, and I was in pain at the treachery my own heart was planning. It had a knife out, ready to stab my resolve never to forgive.

Everyone was so astonished at my outburst they all went silent. Even Father.

I turned to Mother, looking her straight in the eyes. 'Do you *want* to go to Jerusalem?' I asked. '*Not*: can we afford it? Do you *want* it? For yourself? Not for Father, for yourself.'

Her gaze narrowed. I couldn't even hear her whisper. But I could see the word her lips shaped: *yes*.

I turned to Xander and eyeballed him. 'Do you *want* to go to Jerusalem?' I asked. '*Not*: do we have to go by galley? Do you *want* it? For yourself? Not for Father, for yourself.'

Xander hesitated. He looked around, as if seeking escape from my words. Then he confessed: 'Beyond any dream imaginable.'

The brokenness inside me became excruciating. Perhaps I might have been able to resist further if Xander had had doubts, but he didn't.

I went to the woodpile. I found the paving stone that held my secret. Levering it up, I brought out my hoard in its thin leather pouch. It was heavier than I expected.

'What's this?' my father asked as I handed him the grubby bag.

'My running-away-to-Tarshish fund.' I wanted to bawl my eyes out but held myself in check. 'Now a going-to-Jerusalem fund.'

He put down the bag and wrapped me in a hug so strong I could hardly breathe. 'I love you, Rufus,' he whispered.

Xander had opened the bag and spread the coins on the ground. 'It's a fortune!'

No, not a fortune. But enough. I had no idea how much a journey for four people to Jerusalem would cost but, as my heart skipped in a strange beat, I was sure of one thing: it would be sufficient. I felt detached and wondered about the unfamiliar feeling seeping into my heart. Seconds later, I realised it was joy.

I laughed, helpless with love and suspicion. A divine surprise awaited us in Jerusalem at Pentecost. I just knew it.

Murder at my Feet

Cindy Williams

The next morning some Jews formed a conspiracy and bound themselves with an oath not to eat or drink until they had killed Paul. More than forty men were involved in this plot ... But when the son of Paul's sister heard of this plot, he went into the barracks and told Paul. – Acts 23:12-13,16

The afternoon sun blazed on the temple's stark paving stones radiating a heavy heat into the shade of Solomon's Porch. Seated by one of the portico's marble columns, I was practising my writing and observing the people. It would soon be the Festival of Weeks, fifty days after Passover and one of the hottest months of the year. Jerusalem was thick with the heat and thick with the thousands of people pouring in for the festival.

I wiped my prayer shawl over my face. One drop of sweat

would ruin the finely formed letters that marched in Roman straight rows right to left across the parchment. Dipping my reed pen in the inkwell, I started on the thirtieth line.

'Men of Israel, help us!'

The shouts threw off my steady hand. Ink bloomed on the parchment. What should have been a yod, a tiny dot with a tail, was a shapeless black smear. The yod was the smallest letter in Hebrew, as the iota was the smallest in Greek. How many times had I practised both? Every Pharisee student at Jerusalem's great School of Hillel studied the law until they could recite and argue rings around every holy scripture, but only those with the sharpest mind and a steady hand were chosen to be scribes.

'Men of Israel, help us!'

The shouting came from the court of women; men calling to others, sandals slapping the smooth temple stones, outrage resounding off the walls.

My heart picked up pace. The temple precinct was for worship not war. What could have caused such commotion? I pushed back my stool and threw down my pen. The parchment and letters could wait.

I raced across the outer courtyard, up the steps to the terrace and through the gates. The inner courtyard was astir – women whispering and pointing, men shouting and running. I could not see the man they had hold of. A pack of wild-eyed worshippers surrounded him, pushing and shoving and spitting.

The man's accuser stood to one side, his face twisted with indignation and shining with sweat. He was dressed not in the precise garb of a good Pharisee but as one from the provinces

- his cloak too loosely tied, the tassels too short. He raised an accusing finger.

'This is the man who is teaching everyone everywhere against the people and the law and this place.'

'Blasphemy!'

'Traitor!' Men shook their fists and tore at their beards.

'And if that is not enough, he has brought Greeks into the temple area and defiled this holy place.'

A roar went up from the crowd. Women clutched their hands to their hearts. Men tore their tunics. Who would dare bring a Gentile into the temple area? What Gentile who cared for his life would step past the soreg, the waist high wall that separated the Gentiles from the Jewish area? It would never happen.

But the crowd could not think. It swarmed in fury, seizing the man and dragging him towards the gates, towards me. I slipped back outside. My teacher would not be pleased if I was caught in this rioting crowd.

It spilled out onto the terrace. The gates slammed shut behind them, barring the blasphemer from defiling the sacred inner courts. A multitude of hands threw the accused man down the steps and fell upon him with fists and feet and curse words I had never before heard.

Blood pounded in my head. This was murder at my feet. Would I stand by and watch a man beaten to death? Even if he was a blasphemer? My mind was trained sharp as a sword, but my hand had only ever wielded a pen. My heart clamoured in my chest. I had to do something. I grabbed the cloak of an attacker and pulled him away.

'You dog!' His hand hit the side of my head like a hammer.

157

I staggered back, the world wavering before me, and pressed my hands to my head. There was blood everywhere.

'Do you dare hit a scribe?' Fury surged in my veins.

'Go back to your scrolls, boy. Leave us men to defend the temple.' His accent was Asian, the coarse tones of Ephesus.

'As you are letting that man there defend himself?' My blood covered hands were sticky like honey.

'He has defiled the temple. He deserves to die.' The man spat on the ground. 'If you were a scribe, you would know the law.'

'Are you God to murder a man on the word of another?'

'Do you too want to die?' The man's eyes narrowed. His hand slid to his belt. The sun caught the glint of a blade. My breath caught in my throat. In this chaos who would notice him slide a dagger through my ribs.

The drum of hundreds of hob-nailed sandals echoed across the courtyard. Everyone stopped, their hands swiftly stilled at their sides. The man with the knife melted into the crowd. Running towards us, swords and spears at the ready, were centurions, soldiers and the chief of them all, the tribune of the Antonia Fortress.

'Arrest the agitator.' The tribune barked out the order and six soldiers pushed through the people to the battered man on the ground. Hauling him to his feet, they bound him with two iron chains, one around his wrists and another around his ankles.

'Who is this man? What has he done?' The tribune fixed his fists on his hips.

'He's the Egyptian who stirred up revolt!'

'He's an Ephesian – a friend of the uncircumcised.'

'He's the leader of those four thousand Assassins.'

The crowd was in uproar, some shouting one thing, some another.

'He teaches against Moses.'

'He eats with Gentiles.'

'We will learn nothing here.' The tribune rubbed his smooth-shaven jaw. 'Bring him to the barracks.'

The soldiers surrounded the man who was the cause of the chaos and marched him, stumbling in his chains, to the barracks.

The crowd did not disperse. It grew more fervent and furious than ever. Word must have flown through the city for people came running from every direction.

My father's command rang in my ears. *Keep away from an angry crowd. It is as predictable as a winter sea.*

It was true, for the mob had run ahead of the soldiers and streamed up the steps that led to the barracks. They were shouting violence and death, throwing off their cloaks and flinging dust in the air.

'Away with him from the earth!'

'He's not fit to live!'

The soldiers lifted the man on their shoulders and carried him up the steps, fending off the mob with their swords.

Who was this man to cause such commotion? Despite my father's warning, I pushed closer to see. He stood before the tribune, speaking in earnest. His body had not the bulk of a soldier but when he turned to the people and raised his hand, he had the bearing of one. He waited for the crowd to quiet.

'Brothers and fathers, hear the defence that I now make before you.' His voice silenced all but the sparrows: he spoke perfect Hebrew. This was no foreigner or rebel. His accent and intonations were the same as mine: he was highly educated.

'I am a Jew, born in Tarsus in Cilicia, but brought up in this city, educated at the feet of Gamaliel according to the strict manner of the laws of our fathers, being zealous for God as all of you are this day.'

My mouth dropped open. My breath caught in my throat. Gamaliel – the greatest teacher of all Pharisees. Here was a man to be honoured, not attacked. I studied his face. He was from Tarsus, the very city where my grandfather lived. We were a family of Pharisees – my grandfather, his son-in-law - my father, and soon me. I had been raised in Jerusalem and visited my mother's parents only once. Had I seen this man then?

'I persecuted the followers of this Way to the death, binding and delivering to prison both men and women, as the high priest and the whole council can bear witness.' His eyes swept the crowd, settling on the stone-faced Pharisees who stood at the back of the mob. Should they not be pleased that he imprisoned those that followed the way of Yeshua, the crucified teacher from Nazareth?

'From them I received letters to the brothers, and I journeyed toward Damascus to take those also who were there and bring them back in bonds to Jerusalem to be punished. As I was on my way and drew near to Damascus, about noon, a great light from heaven suddenly shone around me. And I fell to the ground and heard a voice saying to me, 'Saul, Saul, why are you persecuting me?"

Saul. The name shivered across my skin. How many Pharisees named Saul were from Tarsus? How many Pharisees named Saul had been felled by a great light? What student of Gamaliel would a venomous mob lock out of the temple? I knew only one: the man who had brought shame to our family, the man we were forbidden to mention. The man that the mob wanted to kill was my uncle - Saul.

***

A thunder cloud loomed over our morning meal.

'How dare he come here stirring up trouble.' My father tore apart the freshly baked bread and smeared on the goat cheese with such force that it flew onto his tunic.' If he would remain roaming the cities of Asia, we could all live peaceful lives. But no! He turns up in Jerusalem like blight in a barley field.'

'Take control of yourself.' My mother passed him a cloth to clean up the mess. 'The Romans have hold of him now. Once they know he is a Roman citizen they will expel him from the city as a troublemaker and all will be as usual. We must keep a calm face - let our friends see that his presence is of no matter to us.'

'Indeed, your brother is dead to us and yet he returns like a shadow to soil my standing in the Sanhedrin.' My father tugged at his beard as though milking a goat.

'Husband, calm yourself or you will suffer not only the shame of a blaspheming brother-in-law but also a beardless chin.'

A smile tugged at the corners of my mouth, the movement sending needles of pain through my bandaged head.

'And you, Eli, look at your face.' My father turned on me. 'Have I not told you to keep away from the rabble? A Pharisee, if he wants respect, must be seen to stand apart.'

'Forgive me, Aba. I did not intend to bring shame to the family. They were beating him to death. I thought I should stop them.'

'Better he was dead so he could lead no more of our people astray. This Nazarene sect is a plague, and your uncle is the ringleader. He stirs up riots among all the Jews through the world with his false claims that Yeshua of Nazareth is alive.' He tore off another chunk of bread, waving it in the air. 'I tell you, if Yeshua was alive, we would have seen him in the temple these past twenty years. A Jew who does not attend the holy festivals is no Jew at all.'

Of our many festivals and feasts, three demanded Jews come to Jerusalem: Passover to mark our people's escape from Egypt; the Feast of Weeks to mark when Moses received the Law on Mount Sinai; and the Feast of Tabernacles, my favourite, where we built and slept in a tent in the courtyard to remember how our ancestors lived during their forty years in the desert. All my friends wanted to sleep in our tent. My older brothers were tent makers in the tradition of the family. They built the biggest and sturdiest tents in Jerusalem.

'How could my brother have fallen so far from the truth?' My mother sipped her mint tea. 'To believe that a mere man could be Yahweh.'

'His followers perpetuated the myth with their empty tomb story, but everyone knows that they stole his body.' My father scratched his head. 'Your brother was more zealous than any in suppressing the conspiracy. Until he went to Damascus.'

'He told the crowd about the great light from heaven that spoke to him on his way there.' I bit into a date, fresh from the palm groves of Jericho.

'Is he still telling that story? Does he still insist it was Yeshua of Nazareth?' My father thumped his hand on the table. 'Let him deceive the Gentiles. He will not deceive us. And you, Eli, stay away from him.'

'Saul was the pride of our family, advanced in the law well beyond his years.' My mother clutched her cup and stared at the stone floor.

'Do not mention his name in this house!' My father grasped my shoulder. 'Eli is the pride of our family. He will restore what your brother took from us.' He held my hand out to my mother. 'Look at these hands. The hands of a scribe. When he completes his studies, he will sit beside me in the Sanhedrin and our name will again be renown in Jerusalem.'

An urgent knock at the door interrupted us. I ran to answer it, relieved to escape my father's grasp. It was the servant of Ananias, the high priest.

'The tribune has commanded a meeting today with the chief priests and all the council. He wants to find out the real reason why the Jews are accusing Saul of Tarsus.' He lowered his voice. 'As you know, the name of Saul has been struck from the official records and must remain so. Yet the rules require that every meeting be recorded. And so, Ananias asks that you, Eli, record the meeting.'

My father stood beside me, chest puffed out, chin held high. 'Eli will be honoured to be the scribe.'

***

I sat at the scribe's esteemed table, my writing implements laid out before me, positioned to hear every word of the council members seated in their half-moon arrangement. The stone-

163

faced Sadducees crossed their arms, surveying my uncle Saul through furrowed brows. The Pharisees did likewise apart from a trio of scribes, my teacher among them.

I sharpened my pen and smoothed out the parchment. My hand was steady, but my insides were a tight twisted rope. I was the first in my class to scribe for the Sanhedrin; I must not make a mistake.

Saul studied intently each member of the council, his oratory certain and strong. 'Brothers, I have lived my life before God in all good conscience up to this day.'

'Strike him on the face.' The high priest, Ananias, bellowed like a bull.

The harsh slap sounded across the room. I started up from my ink strokes. What just cause was there to hit him?

'God is going to strike you, you whitewashed wall!' Saul's lip was split like a grape. He wiped away a trickle of blood. 'Are you sitting to judge me according to the law, and yet contrary to the law you order me to be struck?'

I smothered a smile at my uncle's insult. How many whitewashed walls in the city hid rotten, crumbling structures? What courage, or foolishness, to assault the high priest's purity.

'Would you revile God's high priest?' My father shook his finger at Saul. The council muttered approval at his righteous attack.

'I did not know, brothers, that he was the high priest.' My uncle's words were genuine, contrite. He quoted scripture to back up his apology. I dipped my pen in the ink and kept writing.

Accusations flew like arrows across the room, the Sadducees arguing one way, the Pharisees another. Amidst the arguments,

Saul cried out in a loud voice.

'Brothers, I am a Pharisee, a son of Pharisees. I stand on trial because of the hope of the resurrection of the dead.'

It was fuel to a fire.

'There is no resurrection of the dead.' The Sadducees rose to their feet, shouting at Saul.

'Blasphemy!' The Pharisees leapt from their seats, shaking their fists at the Sadducees. 'You corrupters of scripture. Most certainly there is resurrection of the dead.'

I could not write fast enough. The council had descended into chaos. The tribune and his soldiers standing guard at the doors observed the uproar like iron girded hawks. Was no-one afraid of being arrested?

'We find nothing wrong in this man. What if a spirit or an angel spoke to him?' The scribes from the Pharisees' party stood fast by Saul.

'There are no spirits. There are no angels.' The Sadducees rushed across the room, grabbing Saul.

The scribes pushed them away, dragging Saul from their grasp. They were like wolves with a lamb, ripping his robe, spitting in his face, tearing him to pieces. Were they all mad?

The tribune raised his hand and before I could put down my pen the soldiers were across the room, ploughing through the quarrelling men, tossing them aside. They took hold of Saul and conveyed him from the room, leaving the Pharisees and Sadducees scrambling to straighten their shawls and re-attach their phylacteries to their head.

I rolled up my writing implements. There would be no further call for a scribe today.

***

I selected a scroll from its niche in the wall. Today was my turn to set out the scrolls for the lesson. The students' chamber was large and airy, lined on two sides with a library of scrolls, some papyrus, some parchment, each in their own niche. From these we would recite and argue and debate, imitating exactly the way of our teacher. I touched the cut on my cheek and the bruise that swelled beneath it. Better to draw my friends' questions than their ridicule if I had allowed my mother to dress it with a poultice of honey and myrrh.

Voices sounded outside, murmuring and muttering as they strode past my door. There must have been forty or more. It was nearing the third hour. Why were they not in the temple court preparing for the morning prayer? Why were they hurrying towards the chambers of the high priests? I slipped out behind them and followed. They entered the chamber of meeting, an airy room with windows opening onto the courtyard. I hid behind a pillar and listened through the lattice.

'O teachers of the law, we beg your kindness to hear us briefly. It is regarding the blasphemer Saul, who calls himself Paul. We have strictly bound ourselves by an oath to taste no food until we have killed him.'

My stomach sank like a stone. It was one thing to expel a man from the temple; it was another to murder him.

'Now therefore you, along with the council, give notice to the tribune to bring him down to you, as though you were going to determine his case more exactly. And we will be ready to kill him before he comes near.'

I strained to hear the reply. Surely the chief priests and elders would not agree.

'He is a blasphemer and leads the people away from the truth.'

'Is it not for the good of the nation that he dies?'

I squeezed my eyes shut, pressing my hands to my thundering head. Murder was wrong, more so murder without a trial. Yahweh alone had the right to set the span of a life. Not the priests, not my father. Surely my father was not in there approving. Surely he would stand up for good.

'You again!' The voice hissed from behind, a dagger blade pressed at my neck. My heart caught in my throat. Blood coursed through my veins. I knew that voice. He was the man I had pulled from the crowd, the man with a hand like a hammer, a man hungry for murder.

The morning prayer bell sounded, calling all to the temple. The conspirators and elders poured out of the chamber.

'Whatever you heard, keep your mouth shut.' The man thrust his dagger into his belt and hurried to join them. Only one man looked back. The one man I hoped not to see. His stare struck like a sword. It was my father.

***

I hurried along the porticos, my heart pounding like hooves on hard ground. I had made my decision. I could not turn a deaf ear to what I had heard.

The rabbis commanded I follow them without question. The law commanded I obey my father. To go against them was to be expelled from the temple, from the synagogue, from the

167

family. Yet if I stood by, if I let them kill my uncle, it would be as though I had killed him myself.

I uttered a portion of King David's psalm: *Show me your ways, Teach me your truth.* Yahweh alone knew evil from good. I prayed I was choosing the right path.

The Antonia Fortress loomed before me. Roman soldiers, spears at the ready, guarded the steps like a line of bronze statues.

'I am here to see Paul, the prisoner. He is my relative.' My mouth was dry, my tongue stumbling over the words. Was I mad to willingly enter the enemy's camp? Would they imprison me with Paul?

The cell was not as I imagined – no bars at the window, no chains on his feet.

'The benefits of Roman citizenship.' Paul grasped my hands in greeting, his swollen mouth stretching into a crooked smile. 'You must be my nephew, Eli.'

'How do you know me?'

'A young man who dresses like a Pharisee and looks like my father – you must be the son of my sister. I am surprised your parents allowed you to visit.' The air around Paul was still and cool. I was neither.

'They forbade me to come but ...' My speech tumbled out like stones in a stream. 'There's a conspiracy to murder. More than forty men. Lying in ambush. They have bound themselves with an oath. They have vowed neither to eat nor drink until they have killed you.'

'Are you certain of this?'

'I overheard them speaking to the chief priests and elders. And my father ...'

'Your father was with them?' Sadness swept over his face.

'He was, and I am certain he saw me. If he finds out I have told you, that I have gone against his command, he will disown me.'

'Yet you came.' Paul grasped my shoulder. 'To save men from sinning is always the right way, even if they believe in their cause.'

'I did not come here to save them from sinning. I came to save you from death.'

'And I am grateful.' His battered face broke into a grin. 'Yahweh told me last night that as I have testified to the facts about him here in Jerusalem, so I must testify also in Rome. I would never have guessed he would use my sister's son in his plan.'

'Am I not breaking the fifth commandment – to honour my father?'

'When I was in Tarsus, my father commanded me not to preach about Yeshua. Yet Yeshua himself commanded me to preach about him. Who was I to obey – my father on earth or my father in heaven? I disobeyed my father but I will always respect him.'

'Should I respect my father when he says that Yeshua of Nazareth is dead, that his disciples stole his body, that he is not the promised Messiah?'

'Your father is learned, as I was, yet it was only after Yeshua spoke to me on the road to Damascus that my eyes were opened. Honour your father but search the scriptures for yourself. Every detail of his life and death and resurrection are written in the Law and Prophets.'

'Which scriptures?' Intrigue bubbled inside, livening my mind, inciting my curiosity.

'I do not think we have time for a lesson. Do you not have a murder plot to report?' Paul's eyes danced with warmth and light.

'Read the scrolls of Isaiah and Micah. Then return and we will talk. Now go quickly and tell the tribune what you have heard.'

He called to the centurion.

'Take this young man to the tribune for he has something to tell him.'

***

Soldiers stood to attention, line after line, in the yard of the Antonia barracks. The tribune, hands clasped at his back, walked up and down the rows, inspecting their helmets, their sandals, their swords. This was the feared Roman Imperial Army. These soldiers flogged people first and asked questions later. They nailed people to crosses to remind others to obey. They stopped people in the middle of their work and forced them to carry their provisions and bags. These soldiers obeyed without question and the man they obeyed was marching straight towards me. One word from him and I could be killed on the spot.

'Paul the prisoner called me and asked me to bring this young man to you as he has something to say to you.' The centurion snapped his legs to attention and saluted the tribune.

My legs weakened like water. My stomach churned like the sea. Should I look at this man or lower my gaze. Should I salute him or bow or stand stone still? Two hundred Roman eyes fixed on me.

'I will return in a moment.' The tribune took my hand and led me aside. Two hundred listening ears would not hear from here.

'What is it you have to tell me?'

I recounted the plot, the oath and the ambush. 'And now

they are ready, waiting for your consent.'

'Take heart, young man, today you have saved a man's life. I will deal with this immediately. Now return to your friends and tell no one that you have informed me of these things.'

***

I avoided my father, lingering late at my lessons and leaving home before dawn the next day. I was as taut as a tent rope. A whisper, a shout, the running of footsteps set my heart racing. At any moment I might be hauled before the council. Or worse, at any moment I might hear of Paul's death. Had the tribune been true to his word? Had he saved him?

I could not eat. Raisins stuck in my throat like dried locusts. The day dragged like a slow mule – the morning, the midday, the afternoon prayers. Now at the tenth hour the sun dipped in the west and Solomon's Portico was quiet. I picked up my pen and started once more on the thirtieth line. This time it was not shouts that disturbed me but something far worse – the terse voice of my father behind me.

'Eli, put down your pen.'

Was this the last time I would hold a scribe's pen? Was this the last time I would speak with my father? Would he cast me out on the street? I laid down my pen and stood to face him.

'Son, let me speak plainly. I told you not to see Saul and yet I am certain you did.'

'How did you reach this conclusion?' I countered with a question – my teacher's favoured technique.

'Do you deny that you visited him?' His voice pulled me up

sharp; he had no time for my games.

'How could I ignore those conspirators' plot? Should I stand by and let an innocent man die?'

'Innocent? He is guilty of blasphemy.'

'If what he says is true, if Yeshua is the Messiah, then we would be the blasphemers.'

'Impossible!' He spat out the word.

'We believe we are right. He believes he is right. But he does not plot to murder us.' I too would speak plainly. 'Would Ima be pleased that you were in on the plot?'

My father stepped back as though struck by a stick. His mouth opened and shut, weighing his reply. 'I did not approve but how could I speak against the whole council – and for a blasphemer? Should I sacrifice my standing in the city, the respect of our friends, the honour of our family? We would all suffer - your mother, your brothers, you.'

'Has Paul not lost everything for his belief in Yeshua?'

'If you think he is so worthy, go join him in Caesarea. The Romans spirited him away in the night and are guarding him in Herod's praetorium.'

A yoke lifted from my shoulders. I had saved my uncle. Yet he was still under guard. Would he be safe? Would he be released? Would I see him again? The thought struck me sideways.

I wanted to see him again, to sit at his feet, to hear his arguments for Yeshua of Nazareth. Like a breeze over embers, my heart flamed into life. I lifted my head, straightened my shoulders. A scribe should search out the truth, even more so if it caused people to kill and conceal. The hand of my father was on me – not my father before me but my father in heaven. I would obey.

Meet the Authors

Wendy Adams

Wendy Adams is a retired teacher and mother of four. She has a passion for many things besides writing and reading including martial arts (black belt), running (helped establish her local parkrun) and surfing. Wendy lives on the beautiful north-west coast of Tasmania with her husband and border collie in a small house with a fantastic view of the ocean and the surrounding countryside. She enjoys writing middle-grade fiction and is experimenting with short stories.

D. J. Blackmore

D. J. Blackmore is the author of YA suspense novel *Wish Me Gone*. She also penned adult historical colonial murder mystery *Charter to Redemption*, which was translated into the language of the Czech Republic. Her sequel, *Folly* came next, followed by rural romance *Central to Nowhere*. An advocate for simple living, D. J. Blackmore is a beekeeper and enjoys creating bespoke yarns at the spinning wheel. She has reared Border collies, milked cows and made cheese. But for as long as she can recall, she has been wrapped in the arms of stories.

V. M. Cherian

V.M. Cherian's fascination with stories began at age ten when she first journeyed into Narnia through Professor Kirk's wardrobe. Although she started writing at a young age, she never seriously considered being a writer until recently. She considers her Christian faith to be the driving force in her life. Being a part-time Sunday school teacher, Christian speaker, and a mother of two boys, she loves to write Christian fantasy stories aimed at teaching hard bible truths to children in a magical and fun way. V.M. Cherian works as a microbiologist by day and freelance content writer/blogger by night. She has won many writing contests and completed many writing projects on freelance writing websites. She also regularly contributes to the 'WFC-empowering women globally' Facebook page. She resides in Melbourne with her family. She is currently working on her first Christian YA novel.

Ruth Corbett

Ruth is a New Zealand author residing with her husband in Whakatane.

Books have transformed her life and fired her passion to write material that will encourage readers and deepen their faith. Since becoming a Christian on her 12th birthday, she experienced God's unfailing love and wanted to share it with the world. In response, her autobiography, *I've Fallen in Love* came to birth, followed by a biography *Never Abandoned - A gripping true story of survival*, cowritten with Scotty Saunders.

Discovering *Anne Frank's Diary* as a teenager, sparked a lifelong joy in writing. A love of other nationalities grew through penfriends' letters. Her primary school teaching career evolved into teaching English to speakers of other languages. Before commencing mission work in France, she worked as a volunteer in Israel. Later motherhood became her delight.

She enjoys writing family photo story books, children's plays, poetry, worship songs and short stories.

Amanda Deed

Amanda Deed is an award-wining author residing in Melbourne with her husband, her three grown up children and a menagerie of birds and bunnies. Outside of her family, her life revolves around words, numbers (writing and accounting) and a healthy splash of music. Her first novel, *The Game*, won the

2010 CALEB Prize for Fiction, and she has since had several novels final in the same prize. Amanda loves to write about her favourite things: her faith, Australia, romance and Australian history. As such, her novels explore themes involving spiritual convictions, relationships and historical events.

Anne Hamilton

Anne was a mathematics teacher for thirty years until she became the editor of Australia's most widely read daily devotional, *The Word for Today*. She is the author of over 30 books—ranging from children's picture books to highly awarded YA fantasy and prize-winning devotional theology. If you've enjoyed the story here, look out for her series *Jesus and the Healing of History* —containing short narrative fiction that immerses the reader in the culture of the day and brings insight into how Jesus not only heals people at particular places but also the actual history of the locality as well.

Elaine Hartskeerl

Elaine Hartskeerl has a husband, three adult children and five grandchildren and lives in Melbourne. Brought up in country Victoria by a Methodist minister she developed not only a heart for Australia but a love for God and His word. She trained as a nurse in Melbourne hospitals before marrying and being able to indulge her passion for camping and travelling around Australia.

Elaine spent many fun filled hours reading Australian poets

A. B. Paterson and C. J. Dennis out loud and this is the first time she has attempted to submit a written story to any competion.

Deborah Henley

Deborah Henley is addicted to drinking kefir smoothies, making crafts with her kids and writing stories. She is inspired by her globetrotting adventures, imaginative play with little people and the wonderous things she finds in her garden. Deborah's writing has appeared in a range of publications including *Havok*, *Mum Life Stories*, and *The Dancing Plague: A Collection of Utter Speculation*.

Emily J. Maurits

Emily J. Maurits is a radiographer and assistant minister. She's also the author of *Two Sisters & a Brain Tumour* (a memoir), *Thomas Clarkson: the Giant with One Idea*, and *Olaudah Equiano: a Man of Many Names*. In 2017 she founded Called to Watch, a ministry designed to encourage Christians with chronically ill loved ones. When she's not reading or writing, you can find her swimming (but not through a flood!), cuddling her friends' pets or getting excited about the latest thing she's learnt. An ideal day would involve books, chocolate, moody music, coffee and a cat.

Laura Motherway

From picture books, blogs and short stories, to poems, proposals and post it notes ... Laura just loves to write! A mother of three children, Laura is rarely without a book in her hand, and she wouldn't have it any other way. Laura has spent 17 years developing programs to improve the social and emotional wellbeing of children and young people in hospital, and is trained in Infant Mental Health, Early Childhood Self-Regulation and corporate leadership. She also holds a bachelor's degree in Theatre Arts. She currently works as the Program Lead for the Scribblers Festival in Perth developing an action-packed program of literature treats for the children of WA and is passionate about the important impact that access to quality literature has on tomorrow's leaders, thinkers, and doers. Laura's writing explores themes of home, relationships, belonging and neurodiversity.

R. A. Stephens

Rochelle is a teacher by day, writer, editor and publisher by night. She is passionate about the written word, what stories can do to take a reader to a new world and open our eyes to love, compassion, the bigger picture and much more. When not working, teaching or writing, she enjoys living in the country, spending time with her kids and menagerie of animals, board games and planning what's next. Rochelle is the author of early reader fiction *Riz Chester: The*

Counterfeit Bust and *Riz Chester: The Fingerprint Code*. Rochelle is also the co-editor of *Dust Makers*, *The Opposite of Disappearing* and *Crossed Spaces* short story collections.

Valerie Volk

Valerie Volk has always been a closet writer so, after an academic background in English, History and Education, she retired from teaching and lecturing, and completed two long-held objectives: a PhD and then Master's degree in Creative Writing. Now she writes!

In recent years she has published several hundred award-winning poems and short stories in journals and anthologies, as well as thirteen books, including historical fiction novels, such as *In Search of Anna*, verse novels like *A Promise of Peaches* and *Passion Play*, and biblical fiction like *Bystanders* (2015) and *Witnesses* (2023). She is well known for her poetry collections, like the Caleb Prize-winning *In Due Season*, and *Marking Time*, as well as travel books.

In her very limited spare time she loves reading, film and play going, music (especially opera and jazz), travel and cooking – and the company of friends. But one of the greatest pleasures in her life is simply to write!

Cindy Williams

Cindy Williams writes biblical fiction and historical fiction with a sprinkle of faith. Her second book, *The Silk Merchant of Sychar*, won the 2021 Caleb Award and was a finalist in the 2020 Romance Writers Australia RUBY awards.

She is trained in nutrition, communication, theology, and has a Master's Degree in Public Health. She loves escaping to exotic places to meet the people, learn the history and try the food. She has chewed cow's stomach in China, sampled saltbush (eaten by shepherds and their flock for protein and vitamins) at the ancient ruins of Dor, and drunk sweet water from Jacob's Well in Samaria.

She lives in a sunny nook of New Zealand where she has a love-hate relationship with her vegetable garden. Exercise is her stress relief, prayer is her sanity and coffee and croissants are her downfall.